mindwarp ™

Face the Fear

by

Chris Archer

A MINSTREL® BOOK

Published by POCKET BOOKS

New York   London   Toronto   Sydney   Tokyo   Singapore

This book is a work of fiction. Names, characters, places, and incidents are either products of the author's imagination or are used fictitiously. Any resemblance to actual events or locales or persons, living or dead, is entirely coincidental.

A MINSTREL PAPERBACK *Original*

A Minstrel Book published by
POCKET BOOKS, a division of Simon & Schuster Inc.
1230 Avenue of the Americas, New York, NY 10020

mindwarp™ is a trademark of Daniel Weiss Associates, Inc.
Produced by 17th Street Productions, a division of
Daniel Weiss Associates, Inc., New York

ISBN: 0-671-02168-0

First Minstrel Books printing October 1998

10 9 8 7 6 5 4 3

A MINSTREL BOOK and colophon are registered trademarks of
Simon & Schuster Inc.

Printed in the U.S.A.

Deep in alien territory . . .

Throwing caution to the wind, I bolted down the corridor in the direction of the reactor core. My sneakers pounded the floor in a steady rhythm. I was coming to the door at the end of the hall. As I approached, motion sensors detected my presence and opened the portal for me. I wouldn't even have to slow down—I could run right through it.

That was when I saw the Omega guard standing on the other side of the door.

Desperately I tried to stop and turn around, but my sneakers had no traction on the slick metal floor. Instead of a quick, evasive move I did an embarrassing face plant—right at the Omega's feet! Some master warrior I was turning out to be.

I flipped over, panicked, looking up at my soon-to-be captor.

And relaxed when I noticed that the Omega had six laser rifles slung over his shoulder.

"Cynor!" I said, in the closest thing to a shout that you can manage under your breath. "Boy, am I glad to see you! I thought I was going back into the tanks for sure."

"Ssssilence," he hissed, seizing me by the arms. Before I could react, he had pulled me to my feet, pinning my arms behind my back. "You have been captured. You are now my prisssoner. If you resssist, I will have to use force."

mindwarp™

Alien Terror

Alien Blood

Alien Scream

Second Sight

Shape-shifter

Aftershock

Flash Forward

Face the Fear

Available from MINSTREL® Paperbacks

Chapter 1

Jack

My name is Jack Raynes. I was born in a little town called Metier, Wisconsin, back in 1985. Now it's the year 2118, which should logically make me 133 years old and easily earn me a place in *The Guinness Book of World Records* as World's Oldest Man.

Except, of course, for two small facts: (a) I'm only thirteen, and (b) there is no more *Guinness Book of World Records*.

Heck, there's barely even a *world* left.

Confused?

Hmmm. Maybe I should back up a little bit. . . .

I suppose it all starts with my dad, John Raynes. He died in a plane crash when I was four years old—at least that's what my mom and me always believed. I don't remember much about my father except that he had a scratchy mustache and his hair was coppery red, just like mine.

It wasn't until I turned thirteen that I discovered I'd inherited more from Dad than my hair color.

Now, just like they tell you in health class, thirteen

1

is the age weird stuff starts happening to your body. If you're a boy, your voice changes and you have to begin using deodorant. (And if you're like Drew Molinari, the biggest kid at Metier Junior High, you even have to start shaving. Your *back*.)

Me, I developed more than body odor and a squeaky voice. My blood turned silver, and I discovered I could read and speak any language known to man . . . and even some that weren't. Suddenly I went from being Jack Raynes, class clown, to Jack Raynes, human reference book. And not even a cool reference book, like *The Guinness Book*. Nope, I'm stuck somewhere on the foreign language shelf, next to *Fun with French* and *Let's Talk Turkish!*

Anyway, that was my first clue that my dad wasn't really from New Jersey, as he claimed.

The second clue (and, I suppose, the third, fourth, and fifth) came in the form of my classmates: Ethan Rogers, Ashley Rose, Elena Vargas, and Toni Douglas.

All of them had parents who disappeared on the same day as my dad. All of them had blood that turned silver on their thirteenth birthdays. And all of them had weird powers.

Ethan, who was probably the geekiest kid in school, became this amazing fighter. We're talking *Mortal Kombat* amazing. Judo, karate, kick boxing—it's as if he was programmed to be the ultimate warrior, like Bruce Lee crossed with G.I. Joe. He even has built-in night vision for sneak attacks.

Ashley discovered she had incredible underwater abilities. She can dive and swim like an Olympic athlete, survive in frigid temperatures, and hold her breath for hours. Plus she has supersensitive hearing, like a dolphin.

Toni's powers are even more unbelievable. She can actually suck the energy out of anything electrical and then channel it out of her hands, like a human stun gun. Trust me, you *don't* want to get on her bad side. Not unless you like eating lightning.

Elena developed ESP. Not only could she predict the future, but she could also "astrally project" herself: mentally leave her body and send her spirit flying around through walls and stuff.

You can see why I wish I could trade my powers with any of them. Let's face it—compared to Ninja Boy, Aqua Girl, Electrochick, and Teen Psychic—Translator Dude seems pretty lame.

Even so, you're probably thinking that it would be cool to have my powers. And maybe it would—if I didn't have to keep them a secret all the time. Now, I'm not talking about keeping a secret *identity*, like how Superman is Clark Kent and Batman is Bruce Wayne until it's time for them to fight crime or rescue the beautiful babe.

Trust me, I'm nothing like a superhero. While I'd love to rescue a babe or two, I don't really know much about truth and justice and all that stuff.

Second of all, if you wrapped *me* in skintight yellow Lycra, people would think I was a pencil.

No, the reason we had to stay hidden is because we were being hunted.

You see, our powers weren't the only thing that showed up when we turned thirteen. So did the Omegas.

What are Omegas, you ask?

At first we thought they were aliens. I mean, we'd always just assumed that's what our missing parents were, too. How else do you explain silver blood or the way they disappeared off the face of the earth?

So when the Omegas showed up, we figured they must be some *other* kind of aliens. Enemy aliens. You know, like our parents were Vulcans, and the Omegas were Klingons. The Omegas even *looked* like aliens: tall and skeletal, with large bulbous heads and sinister, jet black eyes. To top it off, they arrived in a UFO. So they had to be aliens, right?

Wrong.

It turns out the Omegas' UFO wasn't a spaceship at all. It was a time machine, sent here from the future. Our parents and the Omegas weren't aliens—they were futuristic *humans*. Humans that had been genetically altered by the United States government to be soldiers in an invincible armed forces.

Our parents, called the Alphas, were the first batch the military cooked up. But they were just the experimental version. They had weaknesses. The government wanted cold, brutal killing machines,

4

and—despite their powers—our parents were still too human.

The Omegas were the next batch. They were designed to be shape-shifters, with the power to change their form to look like anybody and the ability to survive in any climate, even in a postapocalyptic world.

With the Omegas the government finally got what it wanted—and more than it bargained for. Because the Omegas were so brutal, so *in*human, that they turned against their creators. They infiltrated the Pentagon and launched a full-scale nuclear war, destroying humankind as we know it and taking over the earth.

Somehow the Alphas were able to escape into the past, to the small town of Metier, Wisconsin, where they married regular humans and had us kids. Maybe they thought that somehow, by changing the past, they could prevent the Omegas from taking over the future.

But the Omegas must have come after them. That explains why the Alphas faked their deaths and disappeared. That explains why they left their human wives and husbands, and their half-human kids, behind. They probably thought if they were out of the picture, we'd be safe.

They were wrong.

Because once we turned thirteen, once our powers showed up, the Omegas came for *us*, too. And escaping them isn't easy.

Like I said, Omegas have the ability to change

their shape to look like anyone or anything. Your best friend, your teacher, even that loser kid who always sits in the first seat on the school bus. They could all be an Omega in disguise. And you wouldn't know it until it was too late.

Once an Omega impersonated this kid we knew named Todd Aldridge. Todd's dad had also been an Alpha. But Todd had turned thirteen before any of us and was abducted by the Omegas the very same day. So when he turned up again nine months later, with no memory of what had happened, we figured he needed our help. As it turns out, it was *us* who needed the help.

We were nearly captured for being so gullible.

Then Elena *was* captured.

And they would have gotten the rest of us. But we turned the tables on them. When the Omegas trapped Ethan, Toni, Ashley, and me inside the Metier Mall, we escaped the only way we could: by sneaking into their time machine and taking off in it, leaving them behind.

It seemed like a good idea at the time. I guess you had to be there.

Anyway, that's how I ended up here, in the year 2118, running across the surface of an unrecognizable planet that I used to call home. . . .

My breath tore at my chest and the back of my throat. Metier hadn't done too well over the last century. Sure, it was decades since a nuclear war had ended life as we knew it, but the radioactive air was still bitter and difficult to breathe—especially now that I was gulping lungfuls of it at a time.

Everywhere I looked, it was the same: a barren wasteland baking underneath a poisonous yellow sky. You'd almost think you were on the Martian desert if it weren't for the earthly reminders everywhere: hunks of concrete and asphalt. A toppled lamppost. The half-buried skeleton of a building. The rusting shell of a car.

Sure, it *looked* uninhabited. But it was a mistake to think you were alone, that you were safe. Danger lurked around every corner, just waiting for the moment you forgot to—

"Watch your back!" screamed a voice at my side.

I spun as a bolt of red-white laser light exploded behind me with a roar. A minute before, my head had been there. A minute before, a wall had been there, too. Now it was just a pile of smoking rubble.

"Come on, Jack," yelled the girl on my right, "move your scrawny butt! We have to lead this hunk of tin to home base without getting sizzled!"

I turned to glare at my companion. Long curly hair, deep brown eyes, a smile that could make you feel funny inside—not my type, but I could see why some people thought she was pretty. "Is that you, Toni?" I huffed. "From the way you were running back there, I thought maybe it was my grandmother."

"Very funny, Jack," she shot back. "But from the way *you* were running, I thought—"

Her words were cut short as a second flurry of laser bursts struck the ground right in front of us, forcing us to swerve and backpedal, Sonic-the-Hedgehog style, as our attacker appeared around the edge of a ruined building twenty yards ahead of us.

It was a floating metal ball about five feet in diameter, equipped with a single red eye, twin laser cannons—and a bad attitude.

A Sweeper. One of the Omegas' deadly flying robots.

"Wrong way!" I yelled, grabbing Toni by the hand and running back the way we'd come.

The Sweeper streaked after us like a silver snake.

Toni and I bolted out onto a wide stretch of what was once Metier's main street. Our feet flew over the broken pavement in perfect unison, legs pumping like twin sets of pistons, faster and faster.

But not fast enough.

Now that we were out in the open, the Sweeper went into overdrive. It zoomed toward us, its high-pitched motor whining like the world's loudest electric razor. What had been a fifty-foot lead soon dropped to thirty feet, then twenty.

It was homing in, trying to get a lock on our position. I could almost see the little crosshairs lining up in its robot mind. So long as we were in its direct path, we were sitting ducks.

And unless we find cover, we're gonna be roasted *ducks.*

My thoughts were interrupted as the Sweeper's round shadow fell over me. I flinched, feeling the cold, hard edge of fear creep through my body.

Skree-eee-eee-eee-eeek!

With a horrible shrieking sound the Sweeper discharged another lethal rain of blinding rays. They burst in a line behind us, a white-hot trail exploding straight toward our kicking heels.

And then I was hit.

Chapter 2
Jack

"Aaaaagh!"

The scream tore from my mouth before my mind even registered that I'd been struck. Then the pain came: a sharp, burning stab . . . right in my, er, backside.

A laser beam had tagged me, barely, but enough to send me into a sprawling face plant—almost. Luckily Toni's firm grasp on my hand kept me on my feet.

"What was that?" she shouted as we ran, pell-mell, toward a row of dilapidated buildings fifty yards in the distance.

Behind us I could hear the Sweeper's laser cannons recharging. We had fifteen seconds, tops, before the guns would fire again.

"Nothing," I shouted back, suddenly embarrassed. "I'm fine. Keep running."

"But your pants—they're smoking!" Toni cried in alarm.

"Forget about it," I muttered. "We're almost there!"

We had reached the crumbled structures, all that re-mained of a row of old stores: the old pet shop, a beauty parlor, the post office. Now they were just a tangle of exposed girders and blackened bricks. Unfortunately any doors or other entrances were either nonexistent or blocked by towering heaps of debris.

Fortunately there was a narrow gap between two buildings, leading into a secluded alleyway. We darted through.

The air in the alley was cooler than it was out in the scorching sun. But that was little relief as we scrambled back into the shadows, expecting to be blown to bits any second.

About twenty feet in, the alley ended in a solid brick wall, two stories high.

"I'd like to nominate this for a special *Guinness Book* entry," I told Toni as we staggered up to the wall.

"What's that?" she asked, panting.

"Deadest End," I replied, facing the alley en-trance. So far, the Sweeper hadn't followed us. Perhaps the alley was too narrow for it to fit.

"Yours, maybe," Toni huffed. "But not mine."

I turned back around to see that Toni was already climbing up a knotted rope that was hanging down from a second-story window just visible in the shad-ows above us. The rope was old and ratty and looked like it could hardly hold Toni's weight, let alone the both of us. Still, it was the rope or the Sweeper.

The choice was easy.

Grabbing hold of the rope, I scrambled up the thin line after her, careful to keep my hands and fingers away from her shoes. As we neared the top I stole a glance back over my shoulder. Mistake.

"Hurry!" I shouted to Toni as the Sweeper appeared at the entrance to the alleyway, its lasers recharged and looking angry.

Above me Toni's legs kicked out into the air, then disappeared inside the building. A second later I heaved myself onto the window ledge and tumbled through the square opening.

I landed on my hands and knees on the floor of a large, dark room—if you could even call it a room. The walls and ceilings had long ago been knocked out by bomb blasts, and the floor looked ready to collapse. Everything was covered with a two-inch layer of dust.

"Must be the cleaning lady's day off," I commented, rising to my feet.

"Try *century*," Toni added dryly, brushing the powdery soot off her skirt. "Do you think the Sweeper can follow us in here?"

In reply the room grew even darker. We spun toward the window to see what looked like the eye of a giant robotic cat peeking into a mouse hole.

"I think we're about to find out," I answered.

With a shrieking roar the Sweeper launched itself through the window frame. I closed my eyes as bricks, mortar, and wood splinters were thrown everywhere. The windowsill shot clear across the room, landing somewhere in the darkness with a loud crash.

When I opened my eyes, I half expected there to be a Sweeper-shaped outline in the brick wall, like in a Bugs Bunny cartoon. Instead there was nothing but a raw gaping hole, as if someone had taken a big bite where the window had once been.

The Sweeper hovered ominously before us in the dark, its red eye glowing hotly in the dust-filled air. Outside, it had looked large. Inside, it looked enormous.

Toni and I backed away from it, slowly, carefully, our footsteps creaking dangerously across the rotten floorboards.

Spotting us, the Sweeper moved closer. With a soft mechanical whir its laser cannons swiveled right and left, from Toni to me, as if trying to decide which one of us to kill first.

Before it could make up its mind, there was a horrible splintering noise. I turned just in time to see Toni plummet through the floor in a cloud of dust.

"Toni!" I screamed.

"I'm okay," came Toni's choked reply a couple of seconds later. She hadn't fallen all the way through the floor, just up to her armpits. As the dust cleared I could see her straining to hold on to the broken floorboards, like someone sinking in quicksand.

The Sweeper saw her, too.

As Toni struggled to pull herself up, the Sweeper

hovered into position over her, moving in for the kill. Its motor started to rev into the high-pitched whine that I knew came right before a laser blast. I had to do something.

Picking up a broken piece of wood, I chucked it at the Sweeper's gleaming shell. "Hey!" I hollered, waving my arms like a lunatic. "Over here, you big . . . marble!"

The Sweeper spun around to consider me, twin laser guns extending and retracting as it took aim. A hard lump formed in my throat.

"Just a trim, please," I managed to squeak out as the Sweeper moved closer to me, "and a little off the sides."

I held my breath, braced for the worst—

Thweeeeeeeet!

And screamed with terror as a sharp, piercing whistle sounded directly above me. The Sweeper swiveled to see what the noise was—only to come crashing to the floor as a massive web of chains fell upon it from up above.

I looked up, too, and was just able to make out three dark figures hiding in the rafters overhead. They started climbing down from their hidden perch.

Growling like a trapped tiger, the Sweeper struggled to reactivate its hovering devices, rising only a few inches before collapsing back to the floor under the weight of the steel net.

I was about to go help Toni, then saw that she

had managed to climb out of the hole herself. Just as the Sweeper's motor revved menacingly she dashed forward and placed her hand on its metal skin.

"Lights out," she told it.

Toni's hand started to glow. There was a screeching noise as sparks and smoke shot out from under the Sweeper's shell. Then its front panel exploded with a shower of breaking glass, and its red eye winked out.

"And *stay* down," I told it, kicking it with my sneaker for good measure.

"Could you guys possibly have waited any *longer?*" I complained once the three figures who'd thrown the net had joined Toni and me.

"That was great work," said Ethan Rogers, ignoring my sarcasm. "You guys were perfect."

"That Sweeper fell right into our trap," said Ashley Rose, brushing her brown bangs out of her eyes and grinning widely.

Toni grinned back. "Yeah, well, look at the bait," she said, and did a little spin like a runway model. "I ask you, what hardwired Sweeper could possibly resist *this?*"

I rolled my eyes. Toni always got a little punchy after she did her energy drain thing. And after sucking that Sweeper dry, it was safe to say she was literally "drunk on power." Still, it kind of bothered me to see her so perky. Especially since my rear end felt like a grilled steak.

"Oh, please," I groaned. "If it weren't for me, right now we'd be picking you up with a sponge."

Toni stopped spinning and stared at me. "Never mind Jack," she told the others. "He's just feeling a little . . . *sore.*" She giggled.

"What do you mean?" Ethan asked, his eyes flashing with concern. "Jack, did you get hit?"

"No," I lied. "I mean, yes. Kind of. Look, I don't want to talk about it."

"You should let me look at the injury," said the fifth member of our party, a thin, wild-haired boy dressed in skins. "I have healing skills."

"I bet you do, Whistler," I muttered, "but honestly, I'll be *fine.*"

"As long as you don't sit down," Toni cut in slyly.

Ashley's eyes opened wide. "You mean . . . ?" She looked at Toni. Toni nodded. Then both girls cracked up.

"Oh, sure, laugh it up," I protested as my *other* cheeks started to burn—the ones on my face. "Hardy-har-har. Jack Raynes is wounded. What a riot."

"Jack's right," Ethan said, coming to my defense. "It's not funny."

Ashley and Toni stopped laughing.

"You're right," Toni said, sounding guilty. "Sorry, Jack. But you know me. I just get a little giddy when I'm running on full. There was more energy in that Sweeper than I thought. Sorry."

"Yeah," Ashley added, looking at her feet, "that was pretty insensitive. I'm sorry."

"Apologies accepted," I said.

Whistler stepped up beside me. "Well, Jack," he said, placing his arm around my shoulders, "now you know what it means to be the *butt* of a joke."

That was all it took.

Toni and Ashley started laughing again. Even Ethan couldn't hold back this time. As their laughter echoed around the decrepit building I sighed to myself.

I had a feeling it was going to be a *looong* day.

Chapter 3
Ethan

"A perfect specimen!" the white-haired, bushy-browed old man exclaimed, rubbing his hands together with glee. "I can scarcely wait to cut it open!"

We were gathered around an examining table, where the Sweeper had been bound with a series of leather straps. Its chrome surface gleamed dully under the light provided by the thousands of candles that lined the cavernous chamber. They cast their flickering light on the hundreds of shelves that lined the walls, overflowing with books and charts.

We called the old guy the professor. What his real name was, no one knew. What we *did* know was that he was one of the oldest human survivors of the war with the Omegas, one of the smart few who headed underground to avoid the nuclear fallout. The people who my father, the Alpha named Henley, had organized into the Resistance. The people he had given his life trying to save.

Now that my father was dead, the professor was the leader of the Resistance, which had been reduced to a small band of about fifty men, women, and children. Hardly what you'd call an army. Rather than fighting the Omegas, their main concern these days was simply trying to stay alive. Which meant staying hidden.

The room we were standing in was the professor's underground lab, part of a huge complex of secret caves and tunnels that the Resistance called home, made up of the basements of some of Metier's downtown buildings. At one point the lab had been the indoor swimming pool of the old Liberty Hotel. That explained the words No Diving and 8 Feet . . . 6 Feet . . . 4 Feet spelled out in tile on the walls. Looking around at all the professor's books, furniture, tools, and piles of junk that filled the space, it was difficult to imagine that people had actually swum laps here once upon a time.

So far the Resistance had managed to keep their base a secret. The entrance, through an elevator shaft hidden in the rubble up above, was well guarded. It had to be. The Omegas were constantly on the lookout for any human survivors. Using their Sweepers, they had managed to find and destroy the previous ten bases. We all knew it was only a matter of time before the Omegas sniffed this one out, too. Unless we did something to prevent that from happening.

And that's just what we were doing.

It had taken all five of us kids to roll the "dead"

Sweeper back here to the professor's underground lab. At first Jack complained that his injury should exempt him from any further duties that day. From the way he carried on, you'd think he'd lost a limb or something. Of course, once he realized that it was getting dark out, he quickly changed his mind.

Night is when the rats come out.

Even with Jack's help, we barely made it back to headquarters before nightfall. By the time we rolled the Sweeper into the hidden shaft that led down to base camp, the skies had grown inky and a bitter wind had blown up. The cold even seemed to penetrate down to the professor's lab; I was shivering, but that might have been due to the fact that we were about to get personal with a deadly killing machine.

"Are we ready?" the professor asked, blowing a shock of white hair out of his eyes. "Okay, we begin."

With that he snapped a pair of goggles over his eyes and picked up a large, electric circular saw. "Toni?"

Standing a few yards away, Toni nodded. Gathering up the saw's orange cord, she pinched the metal prongs between her two fingers.

At once the saw whizzed to life in the professor's hands. Its high-pitched whine echoed loudly against the tiled walls.

For a second I just stared at Toni in awe. Her powers were truly mind warping. Imagine. The same electricity she had drained from the Sweeper was now being used to cut it open.

Sometimes I wished I could trade powers with one of my friends. Sure, my fighting skills had gotten me out of a lot of tough spots, but that was the problem with them: I had to be *fighting* with somebody in order to use them. Ashley, Jack, and Toni could use their powers whenever they wanted.

The professor carefully lowered the spinning blade to the Sweeper's metal surface. As the saw hit the metal it kicked up a shower of bright white sparks. "There, now," he said as he widened the cut, "this won't hurt a bit."

"How many Sweepers have you dissected?" I shouted over the din.

"This is my first one," he admitted, "but it feels like we're doing it right." He whistled between his teeth. "For instance, it doesn't seem to be booby trapped."

"Booby trapped?" Ashley repeated.

"I was worried it might be rigged," he explained, "to blow up if it's penetrated. But so far . . . so good!"

His words weren't very comforting. All of us kids backed away from the table until the professor's saw had completely severed the thick steel band around the Sweeper's middle.

When he had completed his incision, the professor signaled to Toni. She let go of the cord, and the blade slowly whined to a stop. She yawned, but whether it was because using her power had tired her or because she was bored, I couldn't tell.

Picking up a crowbar and a giant pair of metal tongs, the professor separated the two halves of the shell.

For some reason I'd expected the Sweeper to be filled with a solid mass of wires and circuit boards, like the inside of a computer. Instead I found myself looking at a strange arrangement of interlocking metal rings, like some kind of complex gyroscope.

"What's that?" I asked as the professor pried a black metal box from inside the Sweeper's shell. It was about six inches square, with a red blinking light on top.

"This," he replied, carrying it over to a side table, "is the Sweeper's distress beacon. My guess is it's sending an emergency signal back to the Omega base, telling them that it's down and needs help."

"A distress beacon?" Ashley asked, fear darkening her face. "You mean like an alarm?"

"That's right," the professor replied calmly.

"So they could trace it here?" Toni asked.

"Well, they could," he told her, "if it weren't for the screwdriver."

"What screwdriver?" I asked.

In the blink of an eye the professor lifted a huge screwdriver off the table and rammed the tool down through the blinking box. There was a crunch of metal on metal followed by a shower of sparks and smoke.

"*That* screwdriver," he said, winking at us.

Turning back to the examining table, the professor

pushed aside some of the gyroscopic rings. "Ahhhh, yes," he said softly, tapping with one long, gnarled finger on a brass sphere nestled deep inside the Sweeper's innards. "Now, right here, that's the most important part. *This* is what we came for."

"Is that the Sweeper's brain?" I asked.

"No," he replied. "It's more like its heart. The power source."

"What's inside it?" Toni asked.

"Try to guess," the professor said, lifting out the brass ball. "This little fella has to power that robot's laser cannons, give it the energy to steer, and keep it floating twenty-four hours a day, seven days a week. What do you think could provide that kind of energy?"

"Double-A batteries?" Jack suggested.

"Plutonium," the professor answered. "The key component of a fission reactor or the raw material—"

"Of a bomb," I finished for him.

The professor looked at me and smiled. "Precisely."

Chapter 4
Toni

"A *bomb?*" I repeated, staring the professor in the eyes. "You mean like to blow things up with?"

Okay. I know—stupid question. But I'd just spent the last fifteen minutes acting as a human socket, and that tends to make me a little light-headed.

"Not things," the professor replied, removing his goggles. "*Thing.* Specifically, the Omega dome."

We all fell silent, letting his words sink in.

The Omega dome.

He was talking about the fortress our enemies had erected on the sight of Metier's old reservoir. It was immense, over twenty stories tall and a half mile in diameter. It looked like the Death Star sunk halfway into the ground. And it was impenetrable. The Omegas entered by riding their hovercrafts through a landing port on the roof. The only other way in was through giant exhaust ports that ringed its base but periodically spewed out deadly jets of flame, like dragon's breath.

I shuddered. I couldn't help it.

A week ago Jack and I had actually been inside

the dome by riding in on the back of a Sweeper. (Next to bleaching my hair in fifth grade, it was the stupidest thing I'd ever done.) We barely escaped with our lives. I never wanted to go back. Ever.

Ashley was the first to break the silence.

"I don't mean to be rude, Professor," she said, "but how do you expect to get the bomb *to* the Omega dome?"

"Federal Express?" Jack said. Ashley elbowed him in the ribs.

"How about a missile?" Ethan suggested.

"I've considered that," the professor replied. "But I fear the Omegas' force shield would deflect any rockets aimed their way. No, the bomb has to be planted *inside* the Omega base. Nothing short of that will be of any use."

I suddenly had an idea. "Maybe you could put it back inside the Sweeper. It will return to the dome automatically."

"That was, indeed, my original plan," the professor said. "But this Sweeper has been damaged too much. Not to mention that it wouldn't be able to fly if its power source is converted into a bomb." He paused, as if thinking of something. "Of course, we could always try to capture a *second* Sweeper. . . ."

"No *way*," Jack stated firmly. "I already lost one butt cheek getting *this* Sweeper, thank you very much. I'm not gonna lose the other."

The professor chuckled. "I didn't think so.

Besides, if my guess is correct, once the Omegas realize that one of their Sweepers is missing, they'll suspect that something is up. They'll probably inspect every Sweeper that returns to the dome."

Ashley sighed. "So if we don't fire it in a missile, and we don't attach it to a Sweeper, how do we get the bomb inside?"

"We hand deliver it," the professor answered.

"*Excuse* me?" I blurted.

"*What?*" Ashley exclaimed. "Are you nuts?"

"Not at all," the professor said. Crossing to a shelf, he removed a long scroll of paper, then spread it out for us to see.

"This is a diagram of the water system in Metier Township," he explained, pointing at the blueprint. It looked kind of like a road map, with all the streets leading toward one central location.

"As you know," the professor continued, "the Omega base was built smack-dab in the center of what was once Metier's reservoir, where the whole town got its water. There are still pipes leading in and out of the basin, right under the heart of their headquarters."

"That's *crazy!*" Jack said. "You expect us to sneak a nuclear device into a heavily guarded fortress full of Omega assassins by crawling along pipes that are centuries old and might collapse at any moment? I don't *think* so."

"Well, you don't have to worry, Jack," the professor

27

continued. "The pipes are full of water. Ashley, with her underwater ability, is the only one who could do it."

Jack sighed with relief. "Oh. Okay. In that case, it sounds good to me."

"*Hello?*" Ashley said, in shock. "Just a second ago you thought it was crazy!"

Jack patted her on the shoulder. "Well, that was before I knew you'd be going it alone, Froggy."

Ashley jerked out of Jack's grasp. "Sorry to disappoint you, Jack, but *Froggy's* not going anywhere. Especially not to plant a bomb. And in case you've all forgotten, Elena and Todd are still trapped somewhere inside the dome. If we blow up the Omegas, we blow *them* up, too."

"And destroy the Omegas' time machine in the process," Ethan added, "which is our only way back to the past. Ashley's right. Maybe a bomb's not such a good idea."

"I've got an idea," Jack piped up. "Why don't we just show up at the Omegas' door and knock? Then we wouldn't even need a bomb—the shock alone would kill them."

"That's it!" Ethan exclaimed, startling everyone.

"We knock?" Jack asked, looking surprised.

"We *allow* them to *capture* us," Ethan replied.

"*Someone* here has lost their mind." I sighed.

"Listen, it's perfect," Ethan continued. "We know the Omegas have been trying to capture us, like, forever. We know it's next to impossible to get inside their base. But we *need* to get inside in order to free Todd and Elena and get back in the time machine. So let's give them what they want."

"But if they capture us," Ashley said, "they'll kill us."

"I don't think so," Ethan told her. He turned to Jack and me. "Didn't you two say that you saw Todd and Elena in some weird holding tanks inside the dome?"

Jack nodded solemnly. "And there were four other *empty* tanks next to them, just waiting to hold the rest of us."

"See?" Ethan said, growing excited. "They won't kill us, they'll just add us to their collection."

"And then what?" I said. "We live out our lives like human Barbie dolls?"

"No. *Then* we throw a fast one," Ethan answered. "We break out, plant the bomb, steal on board the time machine, and hightail it out of there before they know what hit them."

"Earth rids itself of the Omega menace," the professor said, "and you get home. The end."

"That's great," Jack retorted, "except there's just one thing. How do we get out of the tanks?"

"Ashley lets us out," Ethan explained. "With her powers she can swim through those pipes in no time at all. She carries the bomb in with her. Then she finds us and frees us. We plant the bomb, escape, and live happily ever after."

"I don't know, Ethan," Ashley said doubtfully. "I

mean, if you three are captured without me, the Omegas might suspect I'd try to come rescue you. They'd be on the lookout for anything funny."

Ethan smiled smugly. "No, they won't. Because you're going to be captured right along with the rest of us. Then, since their collection is complete, they'll never expect you to sneak in and help us to escape."

"*Hello*, Earth to Ethan," I cried. "You're making, like, zero sense here. How can Ashley be captured with us *and* sneak in? It's impossible. She'd have to be in two places at once."

"Exactly," Ethan replied. "That's why we need two Ashleys."

Chapter 5

Ashley

"No way," I told Ethan. "Absolutely not."

"You've done it before, Ashley," he reminded me. "Remember?"

I shivered as terrible images flashed on the projection screen of my mind.

The woods at night. My boots, running over moonlit snow. A tall, pale man with large black eyes. A sign: Danger, Thin Ice. The ground, cracking away. Frigid, inky water. Suffocating. Clawing to reach the surface. Choking. No air. My arms going numb. Something sharp lashing me across the chest. And then, *then*—

"And once was enough," I said, forcing the memory away.

I guess you never forget the first time you die.

"Think about it," Ethan persisted. "You've got the talent. You must have it for a reason. Why not use it?"

"*Talent?*" I said incredulously. "Playing piano is a talent. Juggling is a talent. What happened to me was a horrible, terrible accident."

"Maybe getting split in half happened by accident," Ethan conceded. "But the fact that each half grew back its missing part to make two of you, *that* takes talent."

"None of *us* can do it," Jack added.

"Toni?" I said, starting to feel helpless.

Toni bit her lip. "You have to admit, Ash," she said, "the Omegas would never expect there to be two of you. And Ethan's right. You wouldn't have that special power if it weren't something meant for you to use."

I just stared at the three of them. Sometimes I wished I could trade my powers with any of them. They had it easy. They'd never had to look at their own dead body.

"Look," I said, "no means no. Anything but that. Let's think of another plan."

"But this plan's *good*," Jack whined.

"I know this is hard for you," Ethan told me. "But I don't think we have any other choice."

"I don't believe you guys!" I exploded. "You wouldn't be saying all this if *you* were the ones who had to be cut in half."

The professor stepped forward. "The operation would be performed under totally safe conditions," he chimed in. "You wouldn't feel a thing."

I looked around at their expectant faces. They needed me, and I was letting them down.

Maybe I should just go ahead and do it.

But then I remembered my blue, swollen face—

the face of the *other* me, the me who'd stayed trapped beneath the ice—and knew I'd never be able to go through with it.

"I'm sorry," I told them. "I really am. But safe or not, I am not going to let that happen ever again. End of discussion."

"Well, if that's really how you feel . . . ," Ethan said. Jack sighed heavily. Toni turned away, unwilling to look me in the eyes. The professor's eyebrows seemed to droop.

"Come on, guys," I protested, "I feel guilty enough."

"Ashley's right," Ethan announced finally. "There has to be another way. There just has to be. All we have to do is figure out what that is."

Later that night I lay miserably in the dark, trying to force myself to sleep. My "bed" was a pile of dirty rags that smelled about as good as the bottom of a gym locker. My "bedroom" was nothing more than a hole dug into the wall, off one of the many winding tunnels that the Resistance called home. The room was barely as deep as I was long; as I lay on my back, my feet practically stuck out into the corridor. If I reached my hands up, I could place my palms flat on the rough ceiling.

Am I being selfish? I wondered.

I guessed that I was. I wanted to be like Sarah Michelle Gellar in *Buffy the Vampire Slayer:* brave, smart, hard as nails. But I wasn't cut out to be a hero. Right now I just wanted to be back in a soft bed, in a Wisconsin where you could go to sleep without worrying about whether the Omegas will find you. A Wisconsin where you could go outside without worrying about nuclear radiation, or giant rats, or laser-shooting robots. A Wisconsin where my dad was still around to protect me.

Dad.

I bet he was worried sick about me. I remembered his anguished face the night I'd fallen through the ice as the paramedics fought to revive me. He looked so upset. His expression said, *If anything happens to you . . . I'll die.*

I hadn't told him where I was going the night the Omegas trapped Ethan, Toni, Jack, and me. The night we were brought here, into the future.

Of course here in the future my father already *was* dead. Along with everybody else I'd ever known in Metier. The Omegas had seen to that.

Now I'd never see him again.

Not unless we could somehow get back on board the Omegas' time machine and travel back into the past.

Not unless I followed Ethan's plan.

But every time I considered going along with Ethan's plan, I felt as if my world was crumbling, as if the ground was opening up to swallow me.

Suddenly I realized that it was more than a feeling. The ground was actually rumbling.

It was an earthquake!

No one tells you how *loud* an earthquake is. The roar was like an angry giant bellowing below the earth. Small chips of concrete fell into my eyes. The ceiling was going to collapse!

I tried to sit up, to squirm out of the tiny chamber before the ceiling caved in on top of me. I hadn't appreciated how truly tomblike it was until now. Every shock wave seemed to push me deeper into the narrow cave.

I was going to die. I would be crushed to death right here where I lay. My little bed would be my coffin.

My thoughts were like a scream inside my head: *I gotta get out of here. I gotta get out of here.*

Rolling onto my stomach, I pressed my hands as hard as I could against the side walls and pushed myself inch by inch out of the tight space. Finally I hauled myself completely out of the tiny chamber and into the hall.

Then, just as suddenly as the quake had started, it was over.

For a few minutes I just sat in the darkness, listening to the sound of my heart hammering in my chest.

The professor appeared in the corridor, holding a candle. He was covered in the stone dust that had rained down from the ceiling. I wondered if I looked as filthy as he did. "Are you all right, little one?" he asked gently.

"I guess so," I replied when I found my voice. "I am now, anyway." It was a total lie, but I didn't want him to see how frightened I had been.

"The tremors are deadly, but there's nothing we can do about them," he said. "The Omegas, perhaps we can fight. The earthquakes—they're just something we have to get used to."

"I know," I said.

"I must check on the others. Good night, Alpha child," he said, and continued down the hall.

Watching his light disappear around the corner, I realized that my mind was still repeating the same thought over and over:

I gotta get out of here.

I gotta get out of here.

And right then I made a decision.

Chapter 6

Ashley

The first thing I saw when I woke up the next morning was Ethan's face, smiling down at me. Ethan isn't what you'd call conventionally handsome. I mean, he's not cute or anything. But he has a certain sweetness, and sometimes he looks fierce and sad at the same time, kind of the way Leonardo DiCaprio does. I decided I liked his smile.

I tried to smile back, but my face felt funny. Numb. It was almost like my mouth felt after the dentist's that time I had a cavity drilled. My mind knew my lips were there, but it couldn't make them respond.

Then I realized that Ethan wasn't the only one looking down at me. To his left was Toni, her features fixed in a big, wide smile. Then Jack, with his huge, goofy grin. Then Elena and Todd. Elena and Todd! How had they escaped from the Omegas? I tried to ask them . . . but once again my face wouldn't move.

Wait a second. I had fallen asleep shut up in my cubbyhole. How could they be looking *down* at me? Had I been sleepwalking? I struggled to move my arms and legs, but, as I suspected, they were numb, too.

The others were all just kind of staring at me, smiling those fixed, fake grins. I felt like one of those movies shot from the baby's perspective, where he looks around and sees all the adults staring down at him. What was going on?

That's when I heard the noise.

My ears are supersensitive—it's one of my special powers—so I should have heard the sound long before I did: a terrible whining noise, like a high-powered electric drill.

The whining got louder and louder. My eyes flicked from side to side, trying to figure out where it was coming from. I couldn't even lift my head off the table.

Wait a second. Table?

I was hit with a sudden, terrible realization. I was on the same table that the Sweeper had been strapped to! And I wasn't just numb—I was drugged!

Could my friends have done this to me? No. Impossible. I knew that they were pretty desperate to get back home, but they would never force me to use my powers against my will. In fact, they'd fight anyone who tried to hurt me like this. Still, there was that whirring noise. . . .

Suddenly my friends' faces were drawn away, like a curtain being yanked to either side.

There, towering over me, stood the professor. His eyes had an evil gleam as they reflected the yellow candlelight from around the room. But what scared me even more was what he held in his hand.

The saw.

"Time to make more Ashleys," he exclaimed. He turned around and spread his arms over his head. "Start the drums!" he roared.

A pounding echoed through the chamber. It was beating in time with my heart, faster and faster. The professor was bent over my stomach now. I could see his shoulders and the back of his neck but nothing more. I strained to lift my head, fighting against my numbness, desperate to see what was going on.

Then the noise of the saw changed from the high whine I'd heard earlier to a sickening, wet purr. *What was going on?*

I struggled to sit up, to move, to say something. But I was powerless. All I could do was listen to the deafening pounding and the noise of the saw.

"Ta da!" the professor exclaimed, leering down at me. "Ashley One . . . meet Ashley Two!"

I flopped my head over to the side, following the direction of his gnarled finger. There, beside me, stood my own legs.

He had sawed me in half.

"No!" I screamed, suddenly getting my voice back. "I need my legs! I want them back!"

"It's too late, Alpha child," he replied, and then vanished. I managed to prop myself up on my elbows. Now I saw where the pounding was coming from. There weren't any drums. The pounding was coming from the door . . . and from the Omegas trying to get inside. The wood was splintering under their powerful blows.

I tried to reach my legs, but they danced away from me. "Help," I pleaded. "Help me, please!"

The door fell down.

The Omegas rushed in at me.

And I woke up.

I lay there with my eyes open, gratefully wiggling my toes.

I had never been so thankful to have my body in one piece. I was never going to take my lower limbs for granted again, that was for sure. True, with legs like mine, I was never going to be a supermodel. But at least I could outrun one!

What a bizarre dream. I guess I hadn't realized how stressed out I was. With everything that had happened over the last few days, it was a miracle I hadn't lost it completely.

Pushing myself out of my cubbyhole, I reached over to get my combat boots.

They were missing.

I frowned, looking up and down the corridor. Had someone taken them? They must have.

Rising to my feet, I got a second shock: I was wearing someone else's shirt.

Sometime in the night my own black T-shirt had

been replaced with one of stitched-together leather pelts, like the one worn by Whistler. What was going on here? Was someone playing a practical joke?

As if in reply, laughter echoed down the corridor. It was coming from the direction of the professor's lab. I started walking toward the sound in my socks.

With my superhearing I could pick up their voices: Jack's laughter mixed with Ethan's serious tones and Toni's occasional stinging remarks. The professor's, too. And there was another voice that I couldn't place. It seemed familiar, though. Very familiar.

"Hey, everybody," I said, stepping into the candlelit room.

They were all gathered around the professor's examining table. When they heard me, they all turned around in surprise, as if I was intruding on some private party.

"So what's the deal with my shirt?"

"Deal?" Toni said, staring at me funny.

In fact, they were all staring at me curiously. I guessed they were wondering if I'd changed my mind about the plan. I hoped they wouldn't be too mad when they heard what I had to say.

"Listen, guys," I said, walking over to the table. "I've been thinking a lot about Ethan's idea. You know, about splitting me in two? I really considered it from all different angles. And I decided that although it's a good plan, it's too risky."

Now they were really staring at me, looking totally

confused. Was I not speaking in English? Did I have a massive booger hanging from my nose? Were they just angry? Was that it?

"I know you must think that's kind of selfish, given the situation we're in and all," I continued, trying to ignore their looks, "but I had this terrible dream last night, and it reminded me of how dangerous it could be. The last time I split, one version of me didn't even survive. Plus I lost part of my memory in the divide. That's like losing part of your life."

They all just continued to stare at me.

"For instance, the last time I split, I forgot reading an entire book," I went on. "Who knows what I might lose this time? It could be crucial information. It could be my memories of my mother. It could even be my entire identity. I might wander around like an amnesia victim. The whole plan would be botched. You guys would wind up floating in those tanks forever, and I would never be Ashley Rose again. I don't think we can take the chance. I think we should come up with another plan, one that's truly foolproof."

Boy, did my friends ever look uncomfortable. Toni wouldn't look me in the eyes. Jack was just staring, his mouth partially open. Only Ethan seemed to be listening to what I had to say, although he didn't look upset, as I expected him to be—he looked worried.

"What?" I asked finally. "What is it?"

"You're worried about amnesia," Ethan said slowly, "but you remember who you are *now*, right?"

"And you remember the plan, don't you?" Toni added.

"Yes, *I* do," I said, exasperated. "Of course I do. That's not the question. The problem is that my *clone* might not. Don't you get it?"

"They get it, Ash," said the familiar girl's voice I'd heard from my bedroom, "but *you're* missing part of the puzzle."

Ethan and Toni moved apart, and a figure stepped forward so that I could see her. A figure in my T-shirt. Wearing my combat boots.

A chill ran down my spine.

Because there, standing in front of me . . . was *me*.

"You *are* the clone," she said.

_____ Chapter 7

Ashley One

My clone was now staring at me with a look of shock. I swear, my life just keeps getting weirder. Sometimes I feel like the character in a bad science fiction movie.

"I guess you're right about one thing," I told her, as gently as I could. "The memory loss thing. You don't remember anything that happened last night, do you?"

"I remember the earthquake," she replied in a faraway voice. "And then I had a terrible dream, about being sawed in half. When I woke up—"

It was weird enough seeing myself across the room from where I was standing. It was even weirder to hear her go on like this, in my voice, with my expressions, clearly not understanding the situation.

"You didn't dream," I explained. "Maybe you don't remember things just as they happened. But as for the getting cut in half part . . ." I lifted up my shirt to show her the fading pink scar that encircled my midsection, just above the belt line of my new, leather pants.

"You mean . . . ," my clone started. Then she lifted up her own shirt.

I had the uncanny sense of looking in a mirror. She was frozen in exactly the same position I was. Then she let her shirt fall. "I can't believe you went ahead with the operation," she said.

"Well, I did," I said. *We* did."

"And it was *totally* cool," Jack exclaimed. "The professor was all set to use his surgical tools, but before he barely even cut you, you entered this trance or something and, like, split yourself."

"I—what?" my clone said. I didn't know I could look so pale.

"I've never seen anything like it," the professor added. "Except on a microscopic level. It was like watching an amoeba go through mitosis."

How flattering, I thought.

"There wasn't even any blood," Jack went on. "Where you'd split, your body was smooth and silver, like mercury. Then the silver parts started to grow."

"*She* grew a new waist and legs," Toni continued, pointing at me. "And *you* grew a new head and torso," she said to my clone.

"It must take longer to grow a new head," Ethan weighed in. "You've been asleep for two whole days."

"So," said the professor, holding up the contraption we had been working on when she had entered, "do you feel up for a little swim?"

We waited to see her reaction. Was she going to be okay with this? I hadn't given it much thought beforehand, but unless my clone was willing to go along with our plan, it wouldn't work. I would have split myself in two for nothing.

For a second she just stared around at us numbly. She walked over to the professor and took the bomb out of his hand.

"Sure," she said finally. "Just tell me what to do."

We spent the remaining hours of daylight preparing for our mission. The professor crammed as much knowledge as he could into the time we had left. As a safety measure he decided to send Whistler with us as our guide.

We would be following the old main road past the mall, across the burned plain where Metier Junior High had stood and through the neighborhood where Todd Aldridge used to live, called Goose Hill. It was once the most expensive area in all of Metier, with beautiful three-story houses and perfectly manicured lawns. Now it looked the same as every other part of town: like a cookie pan someone left too long in the oven.

On the other side of Goose Hill we'd find a concrete building that had managed to survive the war with only minor damages. That was the waterworks. We'd know it by the pipes going in and out. They used to be buried, but years of erosion from the heavy winds had laid them bare. Phase one of our mission would be completed when my clone (who we'd decided to call Ashley Two, for clarity's sake) was safely inside the main aqueduct leading to the reservoir and the Omega dome.

I remembered how claustrophobic my little bed had felt during the earthquake and felt a twinge of pity for my clone. If that cubbyhole was bad, the pipe was going to be ten times worse. Once Ashley Two was inside the water main, it would be pitch black and she'd have to swim about two miles—all of it underwater. If she made it through *that* nightmare, there were still the Omegas to contend with in the dome. I felt pretty guilty. Or maybe I felt such an attachment to her that I actually feared for a part of myself. Weird thought. Regardless, if anything happened to her, I felt responsible.

"I've been thinking about it. Do you guys really have to seal up the pipe after I'm in it?" Ashley Two asked. "What if I need to get out for some reason? Like, what if the pipe is blocked and I'm trapped in there?"

We had set out two hours before from Resistance headquarters. Some nights on the bombed-out planet Earth had been totally dark. Tonight we were lucky. An eerie red glow filled the sky, providing just enough dim light to see by. Still, I was glad we had Whistler along with us. Without roads, signs, or buildings my hometown seemed like a foreign country.

Ethan looked at me. I guess he figured I should deliver the news. "If we leave the pipe open," I explained, "the Omegas will know you're in there. They'd hunt you down in an instant since you'd have no way of escape. You'd be captured—and the plan would be ruined."

"Oh," said Ashley Two. The look she gave me had more than a little bit of anger and resentment in it. For a moment I considered offering to switch places with her—but then I realized that being captured by the Omegas and stuck in one of their tanks probably wasn't a much better option.

Suddenly Toni sneezed.

"Gesundheit," my clone and I said at exactly the same time.

We turned to each other. "Hey, that was weird," we continued, perfectly in sync. "Okay. This is totally bizarre," we continued, our voices sounding like one.

Jack, Ethan, and Toni looked at the two of us, surprised. They were silent for a moment. Then they burst out laughing.

"Hey, this is not funny!" Ashley Two and I blurted together. I'm sure the look of frustration on her face was precisely mirrored on my own.

I quickly tried to think of something completely random that my clone couldn't possibly mimic.

"Strawberry cheesecake!" we shouted together.

"The Declaration of In . . . *dianapolis!*"

"Flibber flabber!"

49

"Bloogvart!"

It was no use. And it was more than a little bit freaky. It's one thing seeing your reflection in a mirror or something. It's another altogether to have to deal with a walking, talking duplicate that even *thinks* like you. The sooner we were separated, the better, as far as I was concerned. I could tell from the expression on my double's face that she felt the same way.

"So can I ask you guys a technical question?" Jack asked after a moment.

"Sure," we replied in unison.

"How far does this whole connection thing go?"

I started to reply but held my tongue. Instead I nodded at Ashley Two. "What do you mean?" she asked.

"I mean, you guys have shared memories and all, right?" he continued.

Ashley Two nodded at me. "I guess," I told him. "Up until our separation, anyway."

"So, here's my question. Let's say *you* pick your nose," he went on, pointing at me. "Can she, like, feel it?" he asked, pointing at Ashley Two.

"You're so gross," I said.

"Disgusting," my clone chimed in.

"I mean, let's say *you* get a pimple inside your nose, and *she* has to sneeze—"

"Shut up, Jack!" we said in unison.

"I'm just saying—," he started again.

"Jack, I have two words of advice for you," I told him with a little glance at Ashley Two.

"Oh yeah?" he asked. "What?"

"Drop," Ashley Two said.

"Dead," I finished, and high-fived my clone. I was starting to enjoy this.

"Hey, two against one—no fair," Jack complained loudly.

It sounded pretty fair to me. This clone thing wasn't so bad after all. It was like having a sister, only one that agreed with you on everything.

"Please, you guys," Ethan said, "be quiet. We're almost there."

He was right, I realized. We were just crossing the top of Goose Hill. I thought I could make out the blackened rectangle where Todd's house used to sit. When I was about seven years old, my dad took me there for Todd's birthday party. I remembered that he had a great big dog, and a tree swing, and a pool in the back. I particularly remembered the pool—it was nearly as big as the one the swim team used at our junior high.

A hot, dry wind whipped over the scorched earth, kicking up a swarm of ashes that tasted bitter in my mouth. That was all that was left of the pools, the tree swings, and the homes—a layer of black ash.

"There it is," Toni said a few moments later.

The waterworks was a black silhouette against the red sky. It was smaller than I expected—a building not much bigger than a two-car garage.

Even at this distance I could make out the pipes, dozens of them, snaking away from the one-story concrete box.

And I could make out something else, too.

Omegas.

We all dropped onto our stomachs.

"Great," Jack muttered. "I guess someone failed to mention that it's guarded."

There was an Omega standing to either side of the entrance to the waterworks. They stood at attention, scanning the horizon from side to side. That was the advantage of having soldiers genetically engineered for perfection: They never got tired, and they never disobeyed orders.

These guys had probably been standing in the same spot for days, but they were on full alert. If we went any closer, we'd be spotted for sure.

"Sentinels," Ethan said. "At least two of them. There may be more inside the building. Ashley, listen and tell me if there are more heartbeats."

Ashley Two and I strained to hear any additional noises. There weren't any. "There are only the two we see," I informed Ethan.

"Unless the building is soundproof or something," Ashley Two added.

"If we're going to get inside," Ethan said, "we're going to have to create a distraction."

"Like what?" Toni asked.

"I don't know. Something to lure the sentinels

away from the entrance long enough for us to slip inside, get Ashley Two into the pipe, and seal it up," he replied.

"That's easier said than done," Whistler remarked.

"How do we get their attention?" Ashley Two asked.

Jack smiled broadly. "I've always preferred the *direct* approach."

Chapter 8
Ethan

"*Hola*, Señor Dirtbags," Jack called, grinning from ear to ear. "*Donde está el baño?*"

He was asking them where the bathroom was.

We watched from our hiding place as Jack marched across the charred, pockmarked ground straight toward the Omega guards.

They looked at each other, confused. Jack tried again, in English this time.

"Hey, butt for brains!" he cried at the top of his lungs. "Is it true that all Omegas drink directly from the toilet bowl?"

That did it. Jack turned and scrambled over a hill as the Omegas gave chase. We were lucky these two didn't have their hover scooters with them.

"He's got a good head start on them," I told Toni, Whistler, and the Ashleys. "But we've only got a few minutes. Come on, let's hurry."

We slipped into the darkened waterworks building. It was surprisingly clean inside. Maybe the Omegas intended to use it. I had read how the Roman waterways, called aqueducts, were still used thousands of years after their empire fell. It was funny to think that the same thing might be true for Metier.

"Problem," Toni said, eyeing the array of manhole covers in front of us. "How do we know which pipe is which?"

"It's this one," Whistler said, pointing at the floor.

"How can you be sure?" Toni asked.

"Because that's the only manhole that's been used frequently," Whistler explained. "See how shiny it is around the edges? It's been rubbed smooth because it's been picked up and put back in place so many times."

"So?" Toni said.

"So it's been used the most, and the only pipe they'd bother using is the one that leads back to their base."

"But what if it isn't?" Ashley Two said. "We can't know for sure." She sounded worried, as if she might chicken out at any moment.

We looked at each other. We were all thinking the same thing: *The Omegas are going to be back any second now.* Jack could only keep them away for so long.

"Ashley," Ashley One said gently, "if you don't want to do it, that's okay. I'll go instead. But you have to decide *now*. We can't be here when the Omegas return."

Ashley Two took a deep breath. "Okay. Okay. I'll go," she replied. "Let's open the shiny one."

*   *   *

With Whistler's help I managed to pry up the heavy lid. The thick steel disk must have weighed eighty pounds, easy. We strained to see what was at the bottom of the shaft, but in the dim light of the little building we couldn't make out a thing.

"Ugh," Toni said, getting a noseful of the stale air, "haven't these people ever heard of air fresheners?"

"Are you going to be okay with this?" I asked Ashley Two as she secured the sack containing the professor's bomb around her back.

"I'm trying not to think about it," she replied. "But I guess I'll manage." She started to lower herself down into the black hole. There were metal rungs set into the wall. She got her foot on one, then was on her way down.

Suddenly Whistler grabbed her arm. "Ashley—," he started.

"What is it?" she asked, surprised.

"I just wanted you to know . . . we appreciate what you're doing. It means so much to all of us in the Resistance," he told her.

"I know," she responded.

"So I want you to have this," he continued, opening her palm and pressing something flat and shiny into it. It was his pocketknife. We all knew how much it meant to him—it was the only thing he really owned.

"Aren't you going to need this?" she asked, looking up at him.

"Maybe," he replied, "but maybe you will, too." He shrugged. "I just hate the idea of you down there all alone with nothing to protect yourself. Please take it."

"Thank you," she said, tucking it into her pocket.

"Come on," I warned them, "we have no time to lose."

Rung by rung, Ashley Two dropped down into the darkness until we couldn't see her anymore.

"We'd better get this lid back in place," I told Whistler. Together we slid the manhole cover across the ground with a loud scraping noise. It slipped back into place with a loud clang. *Like the sound of a tomb door closing*, I couldn't help but think.

I looked up to see Ashley One punch Whistler lightly on the shoulder.

"Hey," Whistler said, "what was that for?"

Even in the faint light of the waterworks building you could see that Ashley One had tears in her eyes.

"That was really nice," she told him softly. "I really—I mean, *she* really—needed that."

Whistler shrugged bashfully.

And that's when we heard the screaming.

Chapter 9

Jack

"Aaaaagh!" I screamed as I ran toward the water-works building. "Omegas! Omegas! They're *every-where!*"

With talented acting skills like that, it's only a matter of time before Hollywood recognizes me and puts me in a major motion picture opposite that girl from *Dawson's Creek*. I try to tell all my friends: Get to know me now before I'm too famous to have time for you.

The two Omega soldiers were hot on my tail. We were pretty evenly matched. They had geneti-cally engineered leg muscles, technologically ad-vanced footwear, and a lifetime of military training. I had some old Air Jordans and raw fear.

"Stop!" one of them shouted. "Your running is useless!"

"I know you guys are lonely," I yelled over my shoulder, "but I'm not looking for any new friends! I just don't think it would work!"

That only made them angrier. And I've learned this about Omegas. When they get angrier, they get faster.

Just as I thought they were going to be serving chicken-fried Jack at the Omega cafeteria that night, I rounded a bend and nearly collided with my friends. Apparently they'd heard my warning.

Behind me the Omega soldiers stopped, as if they couldn't believe their luck.

I noticed that Ashley Two was missing. That was a good sign. For one thing, it meant that someone would be able to free us from the tanks—where we were now almost certainly headed. For another thing, it meant that she and Ashley One wouldn't be able to gang up on me anymore.

Whistler was also gone, probably heading back to Resistance headquarters to inform the professor that everything was proceeding according to plan.

I wished I could have joined him.

"Omega base, this is sector gamma-three," one of the Omegas said into his wrist communicator. "We have the targets and are in pursuit. Request immediate backup. Repeat. Immediate backup."

"How many of them are there?" a voice crackled over the Omega's device.

"All of them," the soldier replied.

"Excellent," the voice said. "Do not fail. Reinforcements are on the way."

And that was all I heard as we dashed back over Goose Hill.

According to *The Guinness Book of World Records*,

the fastest land animal is the cheetah, which can reach speeds of over seventy miles an hour. The fastest land animal is definitely *not* the Jack Raynes, particularly when I'd already been chased for a half hour. I was gasping for breath as we crested the hill.

"I thought we *want* them to catch us," Toni panted beside me. "Why are we running?"

"We do want them to catch us," Ethan explained. "But we have to make it convincing. Otherwise they'll suspect a trick. Plus we want to give Ashley Two as much time as possible."

We were on a high stretch lined with rubble now, our feet pounding the packed dirt as fast as we could will them to go.

It was the hour before dawn. To the east the sky was changing from bloodred to fiery orange. Silhouetted against this backdrop were several dozen black specks, coming toward us at a frightening speed.

"More Omegas," Ashley One said. "On hover scooters."

"How are we going to hold them off?" Toni asked. "It looks like there's more than twenty soldiers."

"Make that forty," Ethan said, gesturing behind us.

We turned to look. Our two pursuers had been joined by at least two dozen other Omega foot soldiers, all racing toward us over the ridge. Large metallic spheres hung in the air behind them like a bunch of party balloons. Sweepers, preparing to attack.

I swallowed hard.

This "getting caught" business had seemed a lot easier in the abstract. But now that it was really happening, I was having second thoughts. Was I actually going to let one of those genetically engineered freaks slap cuffs on me, stuff me on the back of a hover scooter, and—worst of all—dunk me in a holding tank filled with yellow goo? I had seen what Elena and Todd looked like in that stuff. It wasn't pretty. What if I couldn't breathe?

But there was no way out of it now. The Omegas had surrounded us. Any sudden move, any attempt to escape, would be pure suicide. I looked over at Ashley One. I could see that the same thought was on her mind:

Please let Ashley Two have made it okay.

And then they were all over us.

_____Chapter 10

Ashley Two

Down and down I climbed. More than once my new leather moccasins slipped on the metal rungs. I missed having my combat boots, but I guess Ashley One was right: I wouldn't need them to swim through a pipe. They'd only weigh me down.

My foot felt for the next step down, swiping nothing but air. I was on the last rung. Darkness below. I couldn't tell how far it was to the floor—or if there even *was* a floor. But I had no choice. Speed was the only thing that mattered. I let myself drop.

I was closer to the ground than I realized. I landed safely, in a crouch, and opened my pack. Everything I needed was right there: my flashlight and the professor's bomb. I switched the flashlight on. It cut through the gloom like a knife.

I was in some kind of control room. A row of old computers, covered in cobwebs and patches of white mold, sat rusting against the wall. I tapped a copper gauge that was supposed to show the water pressure. The needle was stuck at zero—permanently, I suspected. Green crud from the tarnished copper stuck to my fingers. I was probably the first person to read the meter in decades.

Suddenly I got the creepy feeling that someone was watching me.

I swung the beam of my flashlight around and nearly fainted when it lit up the figure of a man, lurking in the shadows against the wall.

Oh, come on, Ashley. Get a grip.

It wasn't a man. It was a suit. Okay, not just any suit. A big, yellow rubber workman's suit, complete with arms and legs, hanging on a peg on the wall. I stepped a few feet closer. There was a tape over the peg. The owner's name, I guessed. Coffy, Lou.

There were other coats next to the first one, all in a neat row. Yakov, James. Lovel, Barnelle. Sizkowicz, John. And a white lab coat, belonging to, I guessed, the guy who ran the computers. Sparks, Thomas.

Thomas Sparks. I wondered what he looked like. I reached my hand into the lab coat, thinking I might find something useful. To my surprise, there was a thin piece of plastic, about the same size and shape as a credit card. His identification. The picture showed a man in his forties with graying hair and thick black-framed glasses but with a kind of nice face underneath them. I wondered if he'd been someone's father. The ID looked about a hundred years old. I glanced at the date. "February 11, 2094." The year the Omegas had launched the bombs.

I had no time to waste. Hiking my backpack up

on my shoulders, I continued past the coats. I climbed down another ladder and found myself in a kind of drainage tunnel.

The concrete tube was about six feet tall and egg shaped; it was round up top and narrower toward the bottom. Water gurgled in a foot-wide stream down the center, but it didn't seem like a whole lot. I had expected the main source of water going into the reservoir to have a much heavier flow. Could this be the same pipe I was supposed to follow?

Icy fingers of doubt crawled down the back of my neck. We had made a mistake. I was in the wrong tunnel. We had picked the wrong manhole.

And I was beginning to get that creepy, I'm-being-watched feeling again.

I wasn't alone. I was sure of it.

Right, Ash, I told myself. *What's sneaking up on you now, a pair of pants?*

Feeling foolish, I pointed the flashlight behind me. Something scurried across my beam of light.

If you're lucky, you've probably never seen a sewer rat in your life. Even if you have, you've probably never seen a giant, *mutant* sewer rat. So let me give you a mental image. Think of a big gray dog. Now remove the ears. Add a row of razor-sharp teeth and bulging red eyes. Lengthen the snout and tail and make both of them the color of earthworms. Give it some black, foul-smelling slime dripping from its twitching whiskers, and you've just about got it.

Of course, I didn't need a mental image.

I remembered something that Whistler was always saying: Where there's one rat, there's bound to be others.

The flashlight beam danced around in my trembling hands. I fought to keep it steady. Raising it higher, I aimed it farther back into the gloom. What I saw was straight out of a nightmare. Hundreds of rats were racing toward me like some angry, hungry flood.

How did they creep up on me like that? I wondered, panicking. With my supersense of hearing I should have been able to hear them from a hundred yards away. *The running water,* I realized. I couldn't hear over it. It was like trying to listen to a conversation in the next room while washing your hands—you just can't do it.

But I could definitely hear the rats now, squeaking in glee as they scented me, their nails clicking on the floor under their scrambling feet.

Thanks for the knife, Whistler, I thought, *but next time I'll take the hand grenade.*

I turned and ran.

There's nothing like a swarm of five hundred bloodthirsty rats at your heels to help you run faster.

I dashed over the slick concrete floor, the pool of yellow light picking out assorted horrors in front of me: rat carcasses, the skeleton of some unidentified animal, an open pit that would drop me into who knows where.

Arms pumping, feet pounding, I ducked into a side tunnel, trying to forget for the moment that I had a nuclear device in the pack slapping dangerously against my back.

This tunnel was narrower than the other one and drier. I actually thought I was making some headway. The rats' squeals sounded much fainter.

I cast a glance over my shoulder and was relieved to see that the rats *were* much farther behind. Their eyes glowed like a million tiny red headlights, bobbing a good hundred yards in the distance.

I just might make it, I thought.

And that's when I ran into the grate.

It came out of nowhere. A thick lattice of black metal bars, stretching from floor to ceiling, preventing me from going any farther. I tugged at it desperately, but it didn't even budge. As far as I could tell, it was cemented into the wall.

I was trapped.

I spun around. The rat battalion was getting closer. I was going to be rodent chow unless I thought of something fast. But what?

The answer was practically under my feet.

There, illuminated in the darkness, was the edge of a metal circle. A manhole cover.

Bending down, I tried digging my fingers in the crack around the thick iron disk. It was no use. They were too fat. I needed something skinnier. But what?

Whistler's knife! I withdrew it from my pocket

and frantically wedged the blade in the crack between the lid and the side of the hole. With all my might I pushed down on the handle.

It was working! The lid lifted a fraction of an inch. Then—*snap!* The blade broke under the pressure.

Almost in tears, I tried it again. This time it had to work. I wasn't going to get another chance—the rats were so close that I could smell them. I rammed the remainder of the knife, broken a little more than an inch above the hilt, back under the heavy manhole cover. Again I struggled to pry out the iron disk, pushing down on the knife handle for all I was worth. The manhole cover shifted a little, just enough so that I could see a sliver of black underneath it.

I quickly jammed my hand under the metal rim. I gritted my teeth against the pain and pulled, my shoulders burning with the effort. Somehow I managed to haul the heavy iron disk up and out of the way. I was home free!

Sort of.

It's true, I'm subaquatic, but no one had prepared me for what I was looking at. There, not two feet beneath me, was a raging torrent of black, filthy water flecked with greasy white foam, roaring angrily as it shot down the underground pipe. If I hit the surface wrong, the water would rip me into pieces. And even if I did manage to get underwater without being decapitated, there was still every chance that I would be mangled and killed by being thrown against whatever rocks, bars, or other hazards were down there.

Of course, I didn't even stop to consider this.

As the first rat leaped straight toward my throat I stepped off the edge of the manhole and dropped into the churning ink below.

_____ Chapter 11

Ashley Two

It was like waterskiing without the water skis. Only worse.

You know that terrible, bitter taste you sometimes get with walnuts? Imagine a hundred gallons of that pumped through your nose at fifty miles an hour. In the pitch dark. The brackish liquid filled my mouth and eyes. I struggled to breathe, choking on the dank water.

That's when I was hit with a sickening thought. What if, as a clone, I only got some of the original Ashley's powers, and surviving underwater wasn't one of them?

I was going to drown.

By now every cell in my body was screaming for air. Suddenly death by rats didn't seem so bad. I'd even have turned back around if it were at all possible. My hands reached out for something, anything, to slow me down. But it was no use. There was no chance I could fight this current for an inch, let alone swim the hundred yards upstream to where I'd started from. Once again I was trapped. This pipe was going to be my coffin.

71

It's funny. As soon as I decided that I was doomed, things got better. It was like something clicked. My body figured out what it was doing wrong, and I was seized by a strange sense of calm.

Just go with the flow, said a voice in my head as the deadly fist of water pushed me down the pipe like a human torpedo. *Just go with the flow*.

I was no longer afraid. The water was my home. I just had to give in and follow my body. It knew what to do.

I was so pleased with my new discovery that I didn't feel the rumbling until it was too late.

Earthquake!

There was nothing I could do. I was stuck in a smooth metal pipe. I just had to take my chances.

The pipe heaved and buckled under the force of the quake. I felt the water rushing at me like a living thing.

Then the pressure started to build.

I clamped my hands over my ears as lines of searing, white-hot pain shot into my brain. It was horrible. So much of the water had run into my stretch of the pipe, passing through on its mad run away from the earthquake, that it could barely fit in the little tube. The pressure that resulted was enormous. My eyes felt like they were being pushed backward into my skull. My body felt like it was in the world's tightest corset. All around me the pipe started buckling and crumbling. *Now I know what it's like to be inside a soda can—just before recycling*, I thought. In another instant I'd be crushed like a Ping-Pong ball under an eighteen-wheeler.

Then with an enormous *whoosh!* of escaping water, the pressure went away. For a minute I just lay on the bottom of the pipe as the ringing in my ears died down. I had made it—I had survived my second earthquake in a week—but I was far from safe. I knew another quake could come at any moment. I had to get out of this pipe.

But when I tried to swim on, I found that I couldn't move.

My left arm had become wedged inside a part of the crushed pipe. The warped metal bit into my wrist like a pair of steel gums.

I tried tugging it. Pulling it. It wouldn't budge.

I was trapped.

For some reason I thought about something my dad had told me once. About how if a coyote gets its paw caught in a bear trap, it will gnaw it off rather than be caught. Actually *chew* its own limb off.

And that's how I got the idea.

I mean, I already knew I could split in half, right?

So what if I just cut an arm off? Would another one grow back? That was my question.

Whistler's knife was right in my pocket. But it was no good, I remembered—I'd snapped off the blade. No way was I going to try a self-amputation with a piece of metal the size of a postage stamp. A wave of nausea hit me. *Am I seriously considering cutting off my*

73

arm? If only a hungry coyote would swim by, I thought, *I wouldn't have to think about this.*

As it turns out, I didn't need a coyote.

Because suddenly my left elbow started to glow.

Have you ever held your fingers over the end of a flashlight? That's what this looked like. Only this light was coming from within me and getting brighter and brighter. I could see the bones inside my arm, long thin shadows running through the center.

My elbow became warm and soft. It didn't hurt. If anything, it felt a little numb.

Finally with a slow, wrenching feeling the upper half of my arm started to pull away from my forearm. My elbow had become . . . gooey. I was nauseated, but there was no pain.

I stared at the operation in progress under the illumination of my separating elbow. It was a lot like pulling apart a piece of gum or Silly Putty—I could even see strands connecting the two parts of my arm. I would have been completely grossed out, but it was like an out-of-body experience with great special effects. The joint itself was stretching but still hadn't given way. Then—with a wet *pop!*—my arm came free.

The upper part of my arm, anyway. The lower part, my forearm, was still trapped.

Don't try this at home, I thought.

A few minutes later I was swimming through the tube. I guess the earthquake had opened up a lot of

74

leaks in the pipe because the current became much slower. It made swimming with one-and-a-half arms a little easier.

I saw a light approaching at the end of the tube. Before I had time to wonder what it was—*shluup!*

I suddenly found myself suspended in midair. I barely had time to tuck my knees to my chest before I hit the surface of the water in the biggest cannonball ever.

They didn't call me Splashley Rose for nothing.

Surfacing, I gasped my first breath of the past hour. Air had never tasted so sweet.

Looking around, I saw that the pipe had shot me out into a huge circular tank. Water poured from three more pipes high up on the tank's curved walls. I glimpsed a ladder set into the wall on the opposite side of the tank and headed for it.

Swimming was difficult without two arms. I was lopsided. It was one thing in the pipe, where I'd just been going straight. But now I was in a tank full of water, which, I suddenly realized, was swirling around. The interior of the tank looked just like a bathtub after you pulled the plug: a fast funnel of water spiraling straight down. I was in a whirlpool! But what was I being sucked into?

I decided I didn't want to find out. I kicked out with my legs, keeping as close to the walls of the tank as possible. The water moved me in a circle like a very wet merry-go-round. As soon as I saw the ladder approach I grabbed for it. Thankfully I caught the metal rung. I would just climb up the other rungs to safety.

That was when I realized. *You need two hands to climb.* But I only had one. All I could do was cling to the cold steel rung as the water tugged at me, pulling me downward.

How long would I be able to hold on?

I'm just going to have to hang in here until I grow myself a new arm, I joked to myself.

I looked down at the remains of my left arm—and gasped in amazement. The patch above my elbow had started glowing again.

As I stared, something began pushing out from my severed elbow. A silvery-smooth mass, like a lump of molten wax. If I hadn't been trying to keep from being flushed down the world's largest toilet, I probably would have enjoyed watching it—like one of those time-lapse movies showing the growth of a flower. Except this was no flower.

Whatever it was, it suddenly started to itch.

I don't know if you've ever had poison ivy. This was about twenty times worse. I wanted nothing more than to rub it with my other hand—but that would have meant letting go of the ladder and getting sucked to my death. I had no choice but to take it.

I writhed and struggled in agony, itching like crazy but unable to scratch. When I couldn't bear it any longer, I rubbed the smooth, silvery extension against the wall of the tank. Finally sweet relief flooded over me. I closed my eyes. Scratching had never felt so good. But when I looked down at what I was doing, I almost let go of the rung in astonishment.

The silver skin was tearing off, like fleshy wrapping paper or a big silver scab. And there, revealed, was a tiny arm and hand—perfect but about four sizes too small. I tried opening and closing the hand. It felt a little stiff, but all the parts worked. I wriggled my miniature fingers. I had a new arm!

But could I use it to pull myself up the ladder? The sound of the water rushing around me was driving me insane. I could barely feel my right arm anymore. My teeth, I suddenly realized, were chattering so hard that it was a miracle they hadn't broken into a million bone splinters. I had to try to get out of here.

With an enormous grunt I kicked hard with my feet. My body rose out of the water, and I tried to grab the next rung with my baby hand. I touched the metal—but it was no good. The new limb just wasn't strong enough yet. I fell back into the water with a jolt that almost caused me to lose my grip on the ladder and go spiraling to the bottom of the tank.

Then I had an idea. Carefully I formed the fingers of my baby hand into a kind of hook. If I wedged it hard enough between the wall and the next rung of the ladder, I might be able to pull myself up. It was worth a try.

Again I prepared myself for the effort. Then with a

mighty shove I kicked off and shot up out of the water. I rammed my baby hand into the space between the ladder and the tank. Then I slowly pulled myself up.

It was working! Holding my breath, I managed to get one leg up over the bottom rung. Then the other. I was standing on the ladder! I was going to be safe!

Slowly, carefully, I started to climb, leaving the raging waters below me. I had a mission to accomplish.

I pushed the grate at the top of the ladder to one side. I was in a cold, dimly lit room. In fact, the only light at all was filtering in through a small round window in the door, like a ship's porthole.

I tiptoed over to the round window and looked out into a bare, gray hallway. Where was I?

I had my answer as two Omega guards abruptly rounded the corner.

I was inside the Omega dome!

If that wasn't enough of a shock, I noticed with a start that the Omegas were leading a string of prisoners. Familiar, thirteen-year-old prisoners. My friends: Toni, Jack, Ethan . . . and me.

I ducked down out of view. No way were they going to catch me now. I'd come too far. I held my breath, making myself as small as possible.

The procession stopped outside my little room. One of the Omegas came right up to the door I was hiding behind. I could see his flat, black boots through the crack below the entry. He stood there for a moment, looking in through the window. Fortunately I was flattened so closely against the bottom of the door that from his angle he couldn't see me.

To my utter relief, he turned away. I guess it was just a routine check. I heard six pairs of feet continue down the hallway—two Omegas and my friends.

Rising, I let out the breath I'd been holding. Once again I'd gotten lucky. Maybe that was another of my secret abilities! Subaquatic, able to divide like an amoeba, supersonic hearing—and superlucky.

It turned out I'd spoken too soon.

"Ashley Rose," hissed a voice in the darkness behind me.

Chapter 12

Cynor

I sat against the wall of my cell, watching the Alpha child react to her name. Surprise. She spun around to stare at me. Her mouth hung open in utter shock.

"Do not be afraid, Ashley Rose," I told her, trying to make my hiss sound reassuring. I knew there was no way that the girl would trust me. She saw me as her mortal enemy. I was suddenly aware of how my voice must sound to her: frightening, hollow, like dead leaves on pavement.

"Don't come any closer," she warned me, although I hadn't moved. Her eyes were wide with fear, the whites showing all around her irises. "I—I have a bomb."

She was brave, this one. I resisted the urge to chuckle. "I'm not coming any closer," I assured her. "I cannot. See?" I held up my hands so that the wrist locks were visible to her. "I am a prisoner, just like your friends."

"You're a prisoner?" she asked, unbelieving.

"Yes, Ashley Rose," I informed her, "this is my cell."

"How do you know my name?" she demanded.

"Do you not remember me, Ashley Rose?" I asked sadly. "That is a shame. But perhaps I can answer your questions like this."

I concentrated, drawing on the natural skill that all Omegas are created with. Energy coursed like static electricity over my body. I felt my features shift into the shape of a raven-haired teenage boy. It was the shape I had assumed on my final mission. The mission that had been my downfall.

"You're . . . Todd Aldridge?" she asked in shock.

"Yessss," I hissed, wearily, "and noooo."

"Are you or aren't you Todd Aldridge?" she demanded.

"How quickly you have forgotten," I replied. "Have my sacrifices meant nothing?"

"I'm sorry," Ashley said. "I'm actually a clone of the original Ashley. I don't have all her memories. Who are you? What's going on?"

I told her the story of how I, Cynor, came to be the first Omega in an Omega prison.

I was programmed to assume the form of Todd Aldridge, the first Alpha child that the Omegas successfully "retrieved" from the past. I was sent back in time to 1998, months after we'd first abducted the real Todd Aldridge. My mission was to contact the other Alpha offspring, disguised as Todd; convince them to trust me; then lure them into a trap. If I was successful, the Omegas would be victorious. The threat of Henley's revolution would be demolished.

What my masters hadn't counted on was that they had made me *too* similar to the real Todd Aldridge. It hadn't been enough to give me the shape of the young boy's body. Any Omega could have simply morphed into that mold. No, in order to fool the Alpha offspring, I needed Todd's memories, his mannerisms, the little "tics" that made him special. In an experimental procedure the Omega neurotherapists had flooded me with the brain patterns of the unconscious Todd Aldridge.

When I awoke, I was part Omega, part human. I had no control over which part of my brain dominated. With Todd's mind came an unexpected side effect: his conscience. Suddenly I felt that it was *wrong* to betray the other offspring, my new friends. When Todd's brain was in control, I could no more lead the Alpha offspring into a trap than he himself could have. For the first time I knew the difference between right and wrong—something no Omega had ever known before.

As you may have guessed, I was unable to fulfill my mission. When my Omega brain ruled, I functioned properly, rounding up the Alpha offspring and leading them to the spot where the mother ship was waiting. But then Todd's mind cut in, and my conscience told me to disobey my Omega commander and free my friends. I sacrificed myself so that the Alpha offspring could get away. The penalty that my fellow Omegas imposed when I returned to the present time was harsh indeed: life imprisonment in solitary confinement.

So here I sat today, locked up in a cell, waiting for the end to come. No one can trust me. I cannot even trust myself. I never know, each morning when I awake, whether I am an Omega . . . or Todd Aldridge . . . or some strange mixture of both.

When I finished, the girl before me looked ready to cry. "What is the matter, Ashley Rose?" I asked her. "Are you crying on my account?"

"I'm not crying," she replied fiercely. Then she continued in a softer tone of voice, "I'm sorry. It's just that I've come so far, and I've been through so much. My friends, the rest of the kids that you guys were hunting, are depending on me to help them. And just when I thought I'd be able to do that, you tell me I'm actually locked in an Omega prison cell. Solitary confinement, with no way out."

She sniffed, trying to hold back the tears. I suddenly noticed that the girl was dripping wet, covered in black filth and not entirely pleasant to my heightened sense of smell. "Did you *swim* here?" I inquired, making no effort to hide my surprise.

"Yes," she snuffled. "I came up through the water main. But we can't go back out that way. There's been an earthquake. The pipe was damaged. The water is still flowing, but there's no way you could swim back through."

"There *is* another way out," I informed her.

Ashley looked around hopelessly. "What do you have in mind," she asked, "tunneling out with a spoon? I hate to be the one to break this to you, Cynor, but I don't think we have time."

"No," I said slowly, morphing from the body of young Todd Aldridge back into my Omega form, "my idea is sssssignificantly fasssster."

Chapter 13

Ashley Two

Whomp!

My strange Omega companion smashed his manacled fists against the door again. He had been pounding at it for almost a minute. "Guard!" he bellowed at the top of his lungs.

I was standing with my back flat against the wall to one side of the door. I was holding the floor grate that I'd pushed aside when I entered the prison cell. It was heavier than it looked, a big square of flat steel. My arms strained to hold it up. The edges bit into my fingers, and my shoulders felt like they were going to rip right out of their sockets. But I had a job to do, and that gave me strength.

"Guard!" Cynor yelled again.

"What is it?" demanded the Omega sentry, appearing at the round window.

"I can't breathe," Cynor told him. "I think I am having an attack."

"What are your levels?" the guard demanded.

"I do not know," Cynor told him. "I need assistance."

There was a sound of the Omega guard pushing

some buttons, then a soft *whoosh* as the hydraulic door slid open. I braced myself—

But the guard remained outside in the corridor. "You are a class-A traitor," he told Cynor. "I am forbidden to give you life support."

"But there *is* one thing you can do," Cynor told him, "and it is not against regulations."

"What is that?" the Omega demanded.

"I cannot speak very loudly," Cynor said weakly. He waved the guard closer.

The Omega guard leaned his head into the cell. *Finally.*

"Go on," the Omega barked again. "What is it?"

"Ssssleep tight," Cynor whispered.

I swung with all my might and connected with an out-of-the-park home run. The Omega's head made a hollow ringing noise, as if I'd struck the bars of a jungle gym. He spun around slightly, then toppled over to the ground. I started stripping the unconscious Omega of its boots and uniform.

"You will find the key to my restraints on his belt," Cynor told me. "Quickly."

Even as I was setting him loose, I noticed that Cynor's features were beginning to change. He was morphing again.

"What a fortunate coincidence," Cynor said, smiling. He was now identical in every way to the guard. He held up the Omega's uniform to his chest. "We are the same size," he told me with a grin.

Rule number one, said something in the back of my mind. *Never trust a grinning Omega.*

But it wasn't like I had a choice.

Moments later an Omega guard led a human prisoner down the corridor toward the captivity tanks. To anyone looking on, it must have seemed like a normal, everyday activity. But as I'm sure you've guessed by now, the Omega was Cynor—and the prisoner was me!

But our scam wasn't entirely comforting, especially since something was bothering Cynor. He looked about *this close* to a nervous breakdown. His hands were shaking as he pushed me along the corridor. And sweat was pouring off his forehead like he'd just run a marathon. "What's wrong, Cynor?" I whispered. "Are you okay?"

"Quiet, prisoner!" he shouted, nodding discreetly toward a security camera on the ceiling.

"Please be ssssilent," he hissed when we had passed it. "If we're viewed talking to each other, they will figure out our plan."

As he spoke, his facial features shifted slightly, becoming Todd Aldridge, before changing back to his disguise!

"Are you sure you'll be okay?" I asked again. "Your face—"

"I will . . . be . . . fine," he replied. "Jusssst, please, be ssssilent."

We were approaching the door to the main prison area. It stood behind six heavily armed guards. I glanced up at Cynor. He was in bad shape. How were we going to get past?

But a moment before we reached the checkpoint, my "captor" pulled it together. Taking a deep breath, he tightened his grasp on my shoulder, pushing me right up to the sentries. "Another one for the tanks," he barked as he walked right past them, never slowing his pace.

"Do you need assistance?" the commander asked him.

"Not with this one," Cynor replied without looking back. "She'll be no trouble at all."

I smiled to myself. If that wasn't the bogus statement of the year. Just wait until they found out how much trouble I was going to be—they'd rue the day they ever set foot in Metier, Wisconsin.

It wasn't until we were safely inside the room, with the door shut firmly behind us, that I felt Cynor relax. His whole body was shaking as he released me from my weird handcuffs. Then he crossed quickly to the instrument control panel.

I was surprised at how empty the room was. Aside from the control panel the chamber was barren except, of course, for the six holding tanks.

They looked for all the world like six big glasses filled with yellowish liquid, stretching from floor to ceiling. I reached out to touch one. It was made of some kind of waxy plastic, clearly strong enough to hold thousands of gallons of fluid but soft enough that I could press my thumb against it and see a slight indentation.

Each of the tubes held one of my friends: Jack, Ethan, Toni, Todd Aldridge, Elena Vargas, and Ashley One. Their eyes were all closed in sleep. At least, I hoped it was sleep.

By now Cynor had entered the right sequence of commands to open the tanks. The room was suddenly filled with a high-pitched humming. The tubes started shimmering, glowing under some hidden inner light. Then to my amazement, the plastic started to part, "unzipping" right down the center. I was surprised: The yellow liquid did not spill out. It just hung there, jiggling slightly, like six huge tubes of gelatin.

If only Jack were conscious, I thought idly, this could be his big chance to get listed in *The Guinness Book of World Records*—as the world's largest Jell-O mold.

"Extraction is almost complete," Cynor whispered, still punching buttons on the control panel.

What more was there? I wondered. I still didn't completely trust our Omega friend . . . partially because *Omega* and *friend* seemed like two words you should never use in the same sentence. Particularly because this Omega didn't even seem to trust himself.

What had happened to him back there in the hallway? If he was barely holding on to his identity and couldn't maintain a shape once he had shifted into it,

91

then he was a risk to our mission even if he *wanted* to help us. It was as if he had a false mustache that kept falling half off. Sooner or later it would give him away. And ruin our plan. But what could I do?

With a hiss like the sound of escaping gas, my friends' bodies started to emerge from the goo. It was as if invisible hands were behind them, pushing them forward. The yellow gel rippled and parted as the six figures slowly squeezed out of its grasp.

Toni was the first to emerge completely. I ran over and caught her body, lowering it gently to the ground. I did the same for Ethan, then the rest of my friends. The yellow substance slid off them cleanly, leaving them slightly damp, like newborn chicks.

My double was the first to awaken.

"Yeeaahhmppphhh!" was the sound she made as I clamped a hand over her mouth just as she tried to let out a frightened scream.

"You have to be quiet," I whispered, "there are guards right outside."

She nodded, and I removed my hand.

"That's the most terrible sensation I've ever had," she whispered. "Like getting novocaine at the dentist, but instead of your teeth it's your whole body that goes numb. You can't feel or move anything."

"I know that sensation," I told her with a shudder, remembering my dream.

"What's the status of our mission?" Ethan asked, barely awake but already all business.

"Well, I'm here, and I've got the bomb," I answered, handing him my backpack. "I think it's okay, but you might want to check it. I had some problems on the way in."

"What kind of problems?" Toni asked, looking concerned.

"Let's just say I could have used a hand," I replied.

"How about the Omegas?" Ashley One asked. "Did you have any problems with them?"

"Not really," I told her. "Luckily I had Cyn—"

"Oh, my God!" my clone interrupted, suddenly noticing Cynor.

Ethan was immediately on his feet in a fighting stance that was only slightly wobbly for two hours in suspended animation. Toni raised her arms, ready to hurl a lightning bolt.

"No, guys, wait," I whispered urgently. "It's not what you think."

"Do not be alarmed," Cynor said.

"Hey," Jack said, scooting behind Toni. "Don't *you* be alarmed, either. Just stand where Electric Girl can get a lock on you."

"I am Cynor," the Omega told them. "We've met before."

"The Omega that helped us escape!" Ethan's eyes flashed in recognition. "Ashley—how did you find him?"

"Oh," I replied casually, "I sort of just dropped in on him."

"I thought we'd never see you again," Toni said. "Did they hurt you when they found out you had betrayed them?"

"We can talk later," Cynor replied. "At this moment we are in terrible danger. The guards may enter at any moment."

"The guards?" Ethan asked, looking in my direction.

"Six of them," I informed him. "Heavily armed."

"That's not our only problem," Ashley One said. She was crouched over Todd and Elena's bodies. "It looks like these two are still out cold."

"They have been in susssspended animation for many months," Cynor told us. "It will be sssseveral hours before they awaken."

"You mean we're going to have to *carry* them?" Jack asked. "That's just great."

"We only have to carry them as far as the time machine," Ethan reminded them. "Then we're home free. Cynor, do you know where they keep it?"

"The chronosphere?" he replied. "It is housed in the launch room, at the center of the dome."

"What's the easiest way to get there?" Ethan asked.

"There isn't any," Cynor replied. "The route is heavily guarded. You have to pass right through the attack unit barracks. Unless—"

"Unless what?" Toni asked.

"Unless you traveled through the vapor ports," Cynor continued, "tunnels underneath the launchpad, designed to carry away the chronosphere's exhaust.

They lead straight from the launch center to the out-side of the dome."

"You mean those *fire tubes?*" Toni cried. "Have you totally lost it?"

As a matter of fact, it did look like Cynor was losing it: Parts of him were morphing back to Todd Aldridge form. His chest heaved with the effort of keeping his guard disguise up.

I knew what was really going on—he was trying to hold on to the Todd Aldridge part of his identity with-out succumbing to the evil impulses of his Omega side. We were in real danger now. If he lost his hold on to his human side, if he reverted to being one of them . . . well, we were already in the tank room. The Omegas' "Alpha baby" collection was complete.

"The vapor ports are perfectly safe," Cynor an-swered. "Unless, of course, the Omegas decide to use the chronosphere."

"Which they only do *all the time,*" Jack said. "I know. Let's just set ourselves on fire now and save some time."

"But if that's the only way to get to the machine," Ethan remarked, "we may not have a choice."

"There's an access tube into the vapor ports fifty yards down the corridor outside," Cynor informed us.

"And how do you propose we get past the guards outside?" I asked. "Just act casual?"

Toni was already headed for the control panel. She placed her hands over the glowing buttons. "As Jack likes to say, sometimes the direct approach is best."

_____Chapter 14

Toni

"Excuse me," I said, smiling my sweetest smile as the door slid open before me with a metallic *snick*. "But I distinctly remember asking for a tube with a *view*."

The Omega guards spun around, drawing their weapons, nasty-looking shoulder laser rifles that I had already seen blast through a solid concrete wall. One thing you had to say for the Omegas: for a society that had no art, literature, or culture, they sure had a lot of different ways to harm you.

I, of course, had only one.

Raising my arms, I launched a tight knot of hot energy at the Omega guards, all the electricity I had just sucked from the control panel. It crackled through the air, hitting them like a big pink cannonball. They hit the ground, writhing and squirming, and then lay still.

We quickly dragged the unconscious Omegas inside the tank room.

I knew they wouldn't stay down for long, and now I was running on low. "We don't have much time," I informed the others. "I suggest we vacate while we have the chance!"

Jack was already dragging Todd's unconscious body out the door. "Way ahead of you as usual," was his reply.

"I'll get Elena," Ashley Two said.

"I'll help," I told her.

"Quickly," Cynor told us, slinging all six of the guards' rifles around his shoulder. "This way."

As we left the Omegas in the tank room I let my hand brush against the smooth metal of the door. A flurry of sparks shot out from underneath my fingertips. "Oops," I said as the metal welded together, sealing them inside. "Clumsy me."

Elena's sleeping body got heavier with each step. I'd always thought of her as such a thin girl, but then, I never had to carry her, while running, through enemy headquarters before. To make matters worse, the shock therapy I'd just performed on those guards had left me drained. If it hadn't been for Ashley Two, I never would have been able to do it.

Man, I thought enviously, *I wish I could clone myself.*

In fact, I wished I could trade powers with any of my friends. Their skills didn't leave them feeling half dead with exhaustion every time they used them. I mean, what good is a mutant power that you have to *recharge?*

At least I didn't have to put up with Jack Raynes's inane comments. He was ahead of us, with Ethan, carrying Todd Aldridge. Ashley One was with them, too.

I was bringing up the rear with Ashley Two and Cynor—*if* he was still Cynor and not some brain-washed Omega. If he'd been having troubles holding on to his identity back in the tank room, they were ten times worse now. His trembling had increased to shudders. *At any second*, I thought, *he's going to blow.*

Finally we found ourselves standing over a smooth metal hatch in a side hallway, an entrance to the exhaust tunnels. "Stand back," Cynor warned, grabbing the latch. "The cover may be pressur-ized." He threw the latch to one side and turned a metal disk like a large, flat doorknob.

There was a gentle hiss of air as the pressure ad-justed. "Quickly," Cynor said, his sides heaving, "there is no time to waste. Hold on to the sides of the ladder as you go down."

I lowered myself into the darkness of the exhaust tunnel.

The air was cool and filled with a sharp, unpleas-ant odor. I had smelled it before. What was it?

"Methane," said Ashley Two, answering my question for me. She had always been the smart one in Mr. Holland's biology class. "It's probably com-ing from the swampland around the reservoir."

"Yesss," whispered Cynor from above us as he gently lowered Elena into our arms. "This tunnel leads directly to the outside."

Once Elena was on the ground, I slumped down next to her. Every surface in the tunnel—floor, ceiling, and sides—was made out of cold, hard tile, like you find on bathroom walls. I guess it was better against fire than wood or metal.

I squirmed, imagining what would happen if the Omegas decided to take their time machine for a spin while we were still in the exhaust tunnel. Would there be any warning? Or would we be immediately consumed by fire, fried in our own skins?

By now the others were entering the pipe.

"*Muchas gracias,*" Jack said as Ashley helped him and Ethan lower the sleeping Todd Aldridge to the floor. "Toni, I'd ask you to help, but I can see that you're totally taken up with sitting against that wall."

Hmmm. Maybe a bath of blue flame wouldn't be so bad after all.

"The launch room is about five hundred yards farther in," Cynor instructed us from the corridor above. "You should have no trouble."

"Aren't you coming with us?" Ashley Two asked, worried.

"No," Cynor replied, "I have something more important to do."

"What's that?" I asked.

"The Omegas will be looking for you," he answered. "I have to—" He pressed his hands against the sides of his head in pain, momentarily unable to speak.

"Are you okay?" I asked.

"I'm fine," he told me when he got control again. Why do people always say that, I wondered, when

100

they are so obviously *not* in any way fine? "You cannot enter the launch room and board the chronosphere without being seen. I am going to create a distraction. Hopefully I can trick the Omegas into leaving the sphere unguarded. When you are sure it is safe, then and only then should you enter the room."

"Are you sure you can manage?" Ashley Two asked.

"I can manage," he replied grimly. He shuddered as a violent spasm racked his body. His breathing came in short, sharp gasps. Finally he regained control again. "Remember. Don't enter the launch room until it's clear."

Then the latch hissed shut and he was gone.

Great, I thought. Our lives depended on someone who at this moment would probably have difficulty licking a stamp, let alone an entire Omega battalion.

"I don't know," Jack said. "Unless Cynor's distraction involves a lot of coughing and spasming, I don't think he's going to be up to it."

"It's risky," Ethan replied. "But we just have to trust him."

We were creeping through the dark tunnel. Ethan and Jack carried Todd. Ashley Two and I carried Elena. My arms were beginning to burn with the effort of moving her. I guess it would have been rude to drag her.

The methane gas was really starting to bother me.

Suddenly I sneezed, nearly letting go of Elena's ankles.

101

"Gesundheit," Ashley Two said. Then she stopped short, looking around as if she'd lost something. "Hey. Where's Ashley One?"

"She's busy," Ethan replied.

"What do you mean, busy?" she asked him.

"I mean she should be almost to the reactor core by now," Ethan said. He shifted both of Todd's legs to one hand and peered at his watch. "*If* she hasn't run into any trouble."

"Wait a second," Ashley Two said. "I'm confused. The reactor core? Why isn't she with us? What's going on?"

Ethan let out a sigh.

"She's at the reactor," Ethan said slowly, "because the professor said that's the best place to plant the bomb."

"When did she leave? Why didn't she tell me?"

"She said she didn't want you to know because you might want to follow. After all your sacrifices, I think she felt bad for bringing you into this—"

"Bringing *me* into this?"

"—and this was her way of making up for it," he finished.

"But she's still coming with us in the time machine, right?" Ashley Two's voice was growing frantic. "I mean, after she's done planting the bomb, she'll join us?"

Ethan winced uncomfortably.

"*Right?*"

"There won't be time," he said. "The bomb is on a

fifteen-minute timer, and the reactor is at least fifteen minutes from the time machine. Even if she ran, she could never cover the distance in time. And that's not even considering all the guards she'd have to avoid."

"So she's just going to let herself get blown up?" Ashley Two was aghast. "I don't believe it. She would never agree to that. *I* would never agree to that."

"She's not going to blow up," Ethan replied calmly. "The reactor is right above the water main. After she sets the bomb, Ashley One will swim safely out of the dome, the same way *you* got *in*."

Even in the dim light you could see all the color drain from Ashley Two's face. "But . . . *she can't!*" she cried. "There was an earthquake on my way in. The pipe is blocked off!"

"What do you mean?" Ethan asked.

"*This* is what I mean," Ashley Two said, holding up her left arm and pushing up the sleeve of her shirt. There was a pinkish, puffy ring around her elbow. And her hand—her entire forearm, actually—looked strange. Kind of glittery. "This is my new arm," she announced. "My old one is back in the pipe, pinned under the wreckage. I had to leave it behind in order to get free. Otherwise I'd still be back there now."

If no one was going to ask her how she had cut off her own arm, I was just fine with not finding out. I mean, there are certain mental images you don't want to keep with you.

"Well . . . maybe the pipe has cleared by now,"

Ethan suggested unconvincingly. "Or maybe Ashley One can clear it herself. In either case, we're just going to have to leave it to her. There's no time to go back for her."

"What you mean is, you don't care if she makes it out or not," Ashley Two snarled. "You're going to let her die!"

"That's not fair," I cut in. "Ethan's right, Ash. We've got, like, *zero* time left."

"Well, maybe *you* guys don't have the time," Ashley Two spat, "but *I* do. I don't care what you say. I'm going back for her."

"There's something you're not thinking about, Ashley," Ethan said quietly.

"And what's that?" she snapped.

"Why do you think your clone volunteered to stay behind?"

Ashley stared at him blankly.

"Because she knows there's no place for two of you back in the past. How are you going to explain two Ashleys to your father?"

"I don't know," Ashley Two started, "but there must be a—"

"And what *about* your father?" Ethan went on. "If you go after Ashley One, there's a good chance both you *and* she will die. If you stay here, there's a good chance at least one of you will survive. Ashley Rose lives on. Your father gets his daughter back."

"Besides," Jack added. "You can always make yourself

another clone once we're safely back in the past."

Ashley Two stared at him with a look I'd never seen before. A mixture of revulsion and anger.

"You think *that's* what it's about?" she demanded. "Ashley One is a human being with all the thoughts and feelings and emotions that I have. That *you* guys have. She can't be *replaced*. You can't just leave her to die!"

"But if you follow her, you risk wiping Ashley Rose off the face of the earth altogether," Ethan pleaded. "Don't you see?"

"No," Ashley Two said, her eyes dangerous, narrow slits, "I don't see. *And you can't stop me.*"

Before any of us could say another word, she turned and sprinted down the tunnel. She was lost in the gloomy distance in a matter of seconds, her footfalls echoing off the tile walls.

Ethan looked off in the direction Ashley Two had taken. "I'm going after her," he told us. "Stay right here. Try not to make any noise." He started to turn away, but then he stopped and came back. "And when I say 'try not to make any noise,' what I really mean is, 'Toni, Jack, don't fight.' If you do, the Omegas will be down here in a second."

Then he ran down the tunnel, leaving us alone in the dark, with Todd and Elena's bodies at our feet. Jack looked down at their sleeping forms.

"Well," he said to me. "At least *they're* relaxed."

Chapter 15

Ethan

I ran down the exhaust pipe as quickly as I could without making too much noise.

I had activated my heat vision. I could see Ashley Two, looking like a glowing white phantom, as she dashed through the round tunnel ahead of me.

It was almost funny. Here I was, trying to save her life. And there she was, *also* trying to save her life. Her clone's life, anyway. It was the "let's save Ashley's life" marathon.

It was strange, the way she had grown so attached to her twin. The way they had bonded. The way one cared so much about the other, enough to risk her own life.

I thought about my last minutes with my father, Henley, before he was killed in an Omega attack. I would have done anything to save him. Even if it had meant risking my own life.

Maybe it was the same with the two Ashleys.

But I knew why I had to catch her: She didn't realize what a risk her twin was taking. The timer on the bomb was set for fifteen minutes. That left no time for mistakes. If I didn't get to her in time, it would be the end of Ashley Rose—both versions.

Just then I saw a faint sliver of light way up ahead. Ashley was opening one of the service hatches, probably close to the reactor core. Then the column of light disappeared, and I knew she had left the exhaust tunnel. She was up in an Omega corridor—and in terrible danger.

I took a deep breath. This was no time for indecision. Running up to the spot where I saw her disappear, I grabbed hold of the metal rungs set into the wall and began to climb.

The metal hatch sealed behind me with a *clang* that sounded as loud as a Chinese gong. As I started to tiptoe down the long hallway the hard steel floor rang with each step I took. No matter how quietly I tried to do things, it seemed like every noise was amplified a hundred times.

How come Nightcrawler always seemed to be able to sneak into enemy headquarters without being seen, smelled, or heard? What I wouldn't have given for a few months' training in Professor Xavier's danger room. I was sure I could be heard at every guard post in the Omega compound.

I scanned the hallway in either direction. No sign of Omega activity. No sign of Ashley, either. Well, at least I knew where she was going.

Throwing caution to the wind, I bolted down the

corridor in the direction of the reactor core. My sneakers pounded the floor in a steady rhythm. I was coming to the door at the end of the hall. As I approached, motion sensors detected my presence and opened the portal for me. I wouldn't even have to slow down—I could run right through it.

That was when I saw the Omega guard standing on the other side of the door.

Desperately I tried to stop and turn around, but my sneakers had no traction on the slick metal floor. Instead of a quick, evasive move I did an embarrassing face plant—right at the Omega's feet! Some master warrior I was turning out to be.

I flipped over, panicked, looking up at my soon-to-be captor.

And relaxed when I noticed that the Omega had six laser rifles slung over his shoulder.

"Cynor!" I said, in the closest thing to a shout that you can manage under your breath. "Boy, am I glad to see you! I thought I was going back into the tanks for sure."

"Ssssilence," he hissed, seizing me by the arms. Before I could react, he had pulled me to my feet, pinning my arms behind my back. "You have been captured. You are now my prisssoner. If you resssist, I will have to use force."

"What's going on?" I whispered. "Is someone listening?" I was hoping he was just keeping up his disguise, but part of me suspected the worst: Cynor's evil side had finally regained control.

My suspicions were confirmed as Cynor raised a communicator to his lips.

"I have Henley's son," he said.

"*Cynor,*" I whispered urgently, "what are you *doing?* Don't you remember—you're on our side!"

I suppressed a gasp as pain ripped through my shoulder and down my back when Cynor increased the pressure on his armlock.

"There is no 'your side,'" he shouted. "There is only our side. Humans are weak, and they must be eliminated." He spoke into his communicator again. "The boy does not have the bomb. We must begin evacuation immediately."

He paused and looked directly into my eyes before continuing to speak into the small microphone. "Evacuate via the chronosphere."

The time machine!

Not only would that ruin our escape plan, but Toni, Todd, Elena, and Jack would be roasted alive! I tried to squirm out of his grasp—and gasped as a second wave of agony washed over my body.

"I warned you, Alpha," Cynor growled. "Do not try to resist, or I will use force."

I wouldn't be any good to anyone with a broken spine. I backed down, going limp, waiting for a chance to strike.

Hopefully my moment would come. If not, I would have to make one.

Cynor spoke one last time into his communicator. "Evacuation begins immediately. Sound the alarm."

_____ Chapter 16

Ashley Two

I stood absolutely still, my back flattened against the wall. In any good action film there's some safe way for the hero to travel. He can crawl around inside the drop ceiling, where the fluorescent lights are. Or squeeze through an air vent on his stomach.

Obviously the Omega architects had never been to the movies.

There wasn't even a doorway for me to hide in: just smooth, metal portals that slid open or closed every ten yards. I was left to walk straight down the hallway, where anyone who saw me could catch me without even a minor struggle.

I had no choice but to hide in plain view. My ultrasonic hearing was turned up just as high as I could get it. If an Omega guard did come down the hallway—well, at least he'd have to run to catch me.

That was how I had found the reactor core: by listening for it. It was the loudest thing in the whole compound, the central power unit that supplied energy for the entire Omega base. I followed my ears until they led me to it.

But when I was almost there, I heard something else: the sounds of four Omega guards, right outside the only door to the reactor chamber. Ashley One must have gotten inside. I was sure that she was in there right now. But how? And how could I follow her?

I could see the Omegas in my mind's eye. By listening for their heartbeats, I could place them exactly on a mental map of the hallway around the corner. They were standing side by side, "flanking" each other. The problem was, these were trained soldiers. Even if I created some distraction, there was no way that I could lure them all away from the doorway.

As it turns out, I didn't have to.

Because suddenly an alarm began blaring down the hall. With my heightened sense of hearing, it was like listening to a jet engine through a stethoscope. I clamped my hands over my ears in pain.

After what seemed like an eternity, the alarm finally stopped, replaced by flashing strobe lights. It was like an Omega fire drill.

Was this the "distraction" that Cynor had spoken about? If so, I didn't have much time to rescue Ashley One and get us both on that time machine. It was now or never.

I took a deep breath. My ears were ringing. I couldn't hear the guards anymore. I took another breath and listened more closely.

Wait a second. Was it that I couldn't *hear* the guards . . . or had they *left?*

I peered around the corner.

Sure enough, the doorway was abandoned. Not believing my luck, I quickly moved to it. I pressed the panel and the door slid open.

The girl with my face spun around as I entered the room. Her expression was exactly what mine would have been at that moment: vulnerable, frightened, tense—but ready for a fight. She stood there in shock, holding the bomb in one hand, tugging at the hem of her black T-shirt with the other.

"What are *you* doing here?" she whispered.

"I came to warn you—"

"Never mind," she cut in abruptly. "Don't explain. You have to leave. It's not safe for you."

"It's not safe for you, either," I started to say.

"Ashley, you have to go *now*," she interrupted. "I've already started the timer. We have less than fifteen minutes. That's barely enough time for me to plant the bomb and get out of here."

"That's what I've been trying to tell you," I shouted. "There was an earthquake that blocked the water pipe! You can't get out that way!"

"What are you saying?" she asked.

"I'm saying that your escape plan is no good. The water main is totally impassable. There's only one chance. We both have to get back to the time machine," I finished, "it's our only hope."

"No way," she replied. "I can't do that. I've got to place the bomb into the reactor core, or the base won't be destroyed."

"But if you take the time to do that, you'll never make it to the time machine! Please, Ashley," I begged her, "let's just leave the bomb here and get out. There isn't time."

"I've come too far," she muttered. "I've come too far, and I'm too close."

She wasn't getting it. She didn't realize the situation. How could she be so much like me and yet so different? Was *I* this stubborn? I racked my brain, trying to think of the right thing to say, anything to say, that would get her to leave.

There was only one thing that might do it.

"What if I helped you?" I suggested. "If we worked together to put the bomb in the reactor, we could cut the time it takes to do the job—"

"—in half," she continued. "And then there still would be time left over—"

"—to get out," I finished. "Exactly."

"Exactly," she repeated. "Well," she said, smiling finally, "let's not waste time arguing."

Chapter 17

Jack

"It's taking him too long," Toni said. "Something's definitely wrong."

Toni and I were still sitting there in the dim tunnel, breathing in the stinky swamp air and listening for the sound of Ethan returning, hopefully with Ashley Two. It had been five minutes since the strange alarm had stopped ringing.

It was still a little painful for me to sit. I just didn't get it. Ashley could grow a whole new arm, no prob. You'd think I should be able to heal a burned butt cheek.

It just wasn't fair. Everybody's powers were so much cooler than mine.

I glanced down at the sleeping figure of Todd Aldridge.

We hadn't even *learned* what his powers were yet, but I'd bet a million dollars they were better than mine. Maybe he could fly. Or had inviso power. Or could make supermodels fall in love with him. Yeah, that was probably it. "So what is it, Todd?" I whispered.

Todd's eyes snapped open.

"What's what?" He yawned, stretching his arms over his head.

I was too shocked to respond.

Suddenly Todd seemed to realize he was lying in a cold, dark tunnel. He sat straight up, looking frightened. "Where am I?" he said, sounding scared. "Who's there?"

"It's me, Toni Douglas," she told him in a soothing voice, "and Jack Raynes. And right now you're—"

"Jack Raynes!" Todd shouted. "Is this another one of your practical jokes?"

"Shhh!" I told him bitterly. "Todd, you really have to keep it dow—"

"I want to know what's going on!" he hollered. "Somebody mmmmph—"

I clamped my hand over his mouth. "Todd, I'll tell you everything you want to know," I whispered through my clenched teeth. "But you can't scream. Okay?" He nodded. "So I'm going to take my hand off your mouth, and you're just going to be quiet so that I can explain things. Do we have a deal?"

He nodded again.

"Great." I removed my hand.

"Help!" he screamed. *"Somebody hel—"*

Suddenly his body stiffened and then went limp. He was out cold.

"Sorry," Toni whispered to me, removing her hand from Todd's neck. "I didn't know what else to do. He was getting too loud."

"Someday, Toni," I said enviously, "you have to show me how to do that human stun-gun trick. I'll teach you any language you—"

"*Shhh!*" Toni hissed as the sound of footsteps grew louder overhead. Too many to be our returning friends.

Omegas. They must have heard Todd's shouting.

I watched Toni's eyes grow wide in fright as the footsteps thundered toward us—hundreds of them, sounding like a stampede of elephants. But rather than stop at the service hatch above us, they continued running right past it, like a passing storm cloud.

Soon the footsteps faded altogether, disappearing in the direction of the launch center.

I let out a sigh of relief. "*That* was a close one," I said.

Toni said nothing. She just rose to her feet, grabbed Elena by the ankles, and started dragging the sleeping girl along the tunnel, leaving Todd and me behind.

"Hey! What are you doing?" I called after her. I jabbed my thumb over my shoulder. "The time machine is *that* way."

"Yeah," Toni called back to me. "And the Omegas were heading that way." Her voice sounded strange. Weak . . . strangled . . . *terrified*.

"Don't you get it, Jack? *They're going to blast off.*"

Chapter 18

Ethan

"Why are you doing this, Cynor?" I asked as my captor escorted me roughly along the corridor. Emergency lights flashed like strobes all around us, signaling the evacuation. I could hear the sounds of Omegas running all around the compound. "Why are you helping the people who locked you up for life? *Why*, Cynor—"

The Omega threw me to the ground. I stumbled, desperately reaching out for something to break my fall. There wasn't anything—the walls of the hallway were smooth as glass. I fell into a kneeling position, hard. Pain shot through my kneecaps and up my legs.

"I am Omega unit 2-0065. There is no Cynor any longer. Names are for the weak."

He jerked me back to my feet.

We were almost at the door to the launch center. All I needed was a break—if I could catch him off guard, or talk him into freeing me, or *anything*. "Okay," I told him, trying to sound reasonable. "You're not Cynor. There is no Cynor. But you still have a past, don't you? And in the past you risked your life to save me and my friends. Why throw that away now?"

"That was an error," he said mechanically, "resulting from faulty neural programming. I will not make that mistake again."

The door was right in front of us. Inside would be about a hundred Omegas, all heavily armed. No chance for escape. It was my last chance. I spun around, looking Cynor right in the eyes. "Todd!" I shouted. "I know you're in there somewhere! How can you let him do this?"

My captor grabbed my shoulders and slammed me into a wall hard enough to knock the breath out of me. His eyes were blazing. "There is no Todd Aldridge," he hissed. "There is no Cynor. There is only Omega unit 2-0065. I will complete my assignment: to eliminate you and the rest of the Alpha offspring. Now, *move!*"

He pushed me through the opening portal and into what I knew was certain death.

_____ Chapter 19
Ashley One

My clone and I were quite a team.

Using what was left of Whistler's knife, we had already managed to loosen one of the metal panels from the side of the reactor core: a large, cylindrical drum that pulsated with an eerie, alien glow. All sorts of tubes snaked out of the top of it like Medusa's hair. It almost seemed alive somehow.

But not for long, I thought, casting a glance at the professor's bomb.

The timer read 00:11:31 . . . 30 . . . 29 . . .

I swallowed hard. _We're cutting it close_, I said to myself. _We're not going to make it._

"We're gonna make it," Ashley Two said, as if reading my mind. "We can do this."

She smiled at me, but it was a quick, nervous smile. I felt the same look flicker across my face.

I had to admit, at first I had been angry when my clone had showed up in the reactor room. But now I was thankful. By myself there was no way I could have planted the bomb in time.

I didn't know if two heads were necessarily better

121

than one. But four hands were *definitely* faster than two.

Finally the metal plate was pried free, clattering to the floor.

My clone and I weren't expecting the intense light that emanated from within the core. It was as if a piece of the sun was contained inside the giant metal cylinder. We had to squint at the blinding white light that streamed out of the rectangular opening.

We bent down to pick up the bomb, raised it to the glowing opening—

And somehow triggered a booby trap.

Before we could react, a solid steel security door slid shut over the door behind us. With a loud, horrible *clank* bolts slid into place, locking it shut for all time.

For a tense moment my clone and I stood, frozen in place, as three small words played through both our brains:

No way out.

"What are we going to do?" she asked me finally, faintly.

"The only thing we *can* do," I answered.

I stared her in her eyes. In *my* eyes. We didn't have to talk anymore. We had no need for words.

Ashley Two nodded at me, then took my hand in her own. It fit perfectly.

It was ironic. My entire life, I'd felt like no one truly understood me. Now, finally, I was standing right next to someone who did.

We turned into the blinding white light.

Together we threw the bomb inside the core.

_____ Chapter 20

Ethan

"Do not try anything foolish, Henley's son," my captor told me. "If you do, I will have no choice but to end your life."

Like I care, I thought bitterly.

We were in the launch center, waiting to board the time machine—what Cynor referred to as the chronosphere. It loomed before us, looking just as I remembered it: a giant silver orb, supported on six spindly legs like a monstrous, crouching beetle. Two neat rows of Omegas were moving in swift military formation into a hatchway in the underside of the craft.

With my hands pinned behind my back, I couldn't see my watch, but it didn't matter. In a matter of minutes the whole compound would go up in a fireball of blistering force. Anyone not on the time machine would be smashed into atoms by the force of the professor's bomb.

My gaze fell to the base of the launchpad, a metal grid with darkness underneath. I knew that somewhere in that darkness, Toni and Jack were waiting with the unconscious bodies of Todd and Elena. Waiting for a

123

"diversion" from Cynor that now would never come.

Should I point out my friends' hiding space to the Omegas? I wondered. Which was the better fate: being captured or being burned alive? A long, numbed life in the Omegas' tanks or a swift, torturous death in a raging inferno?

I wrestled with my conscience as Cynor pushed me toward the ramp leading up to the ship. Last chance. If I was going to blow the whistle on my friends, now was the time. I knew it was an important decision. I knew I had to make up my mind. And I realized . . . I couldn't do it.

Even if it would save their lives, I just couldn't hand them over to the enemy.

Above us, above the chronosphere, the domed ceiling began to open with a loud electric hum, revealing a sliver of poison yellow storm clouds swirling in the sky beyond.

Then something strange happened.

With a horrible *clang* the ceiling crashed shut. All around the perimeter of the launch room the lights exploded, sending showers of glass raining below.

And everything went pitch black.

"Power failure!" an Omegan voice shouted in the darkness to my left.

"Switch to auxiliary!" a second voice called.

There was a sound behind me like a bug being zapped, and I heard Cynor cry out as his hold loosened on my wrists. Suddenly I was jerked out of

Cynor's grasp altogether, and someone was pulling me through the darkness.

"Auxiliary is priming. Stay calm. Everyone stand where you are," a third Omega voice barked.

And then a more pleasing voice, a girl's voice, was whispering in my ear. "Sorry, Mr. Rogers," it said. "But I'm afraid your flight has been canceled."

By now my thermal vision had clicked into gear, and I could make out the figure who was dragging me down into the space beneath the launchpad.

"Toni!" I whispered. "How did you—"

"Never mind," she answered, "let's just get out of here!"

"How long until the bomb blows?" Toni asked once we were in the tunnel. We sprinted down the tube, our feet pounding on the slick tiles.

I checked my watch. "Less than two minutes," I replied. "How long until they get the time machine running again?"

"Not long," Toni replied. "I couldn't drain all the energy out of it. It was like trying to drink the biggest glass of water in the world."

"The world's biggest glass of water was drunk by Rally McCormack of Abilene, Texas," Jack said, suddenly beside us.

Leave it to Jack. Even in the face of death he was spouting useless trivia.

"Where are Todd and Elena?" I huffed.

"Where *we* should be," Jack answered. "Outside."

He pointed up ahead to where a disk of daylight was glowing like the entrance to heaven. Fifty yards to go. Could we make it?

We put on a fresh burst of speed just as a faint humming started up behind us. A low mechanical burr that started rising steadily in pitch, growing louder and louder.

We all knew that sound.

"Oh, God," Toni cried. "Tell me that's not what I think it is."

I glanced back over my shoulder. And immediately wished I hadn't.

Barreling down the tube was a solid wall of flame. The blue-white fire was racing straight at us—at about a hundred miles an hour.

"*Run!*" we screamed simultaneously.

By now there were only fifteen feet between us and the mouth of the tunnel, but it might as well have been fifteen *hundred* feet.

Because we were suddenly whipped backward as all the oxygen ahead of us was sucked into the inferno behind us. The breath was literally ripped from our lungs. We couldn't have screamed if we wanted to.

As my feet left the floor I shut my eyes tightly, not wanting my last sensation to be my eyeballs melting in my own head.

I don't remember what happened next.

What I do remember is an acrid, burning taste in my mouth, followed by a wash of pure heat on my back, hotter than anything I'd ever felt. Then being blasted forward, like a twig in a leaf blower.

I opened my eyes and saw the mouth of the tunnel whip past me—and then suddenly the ground, looking as if it was hundreds of feet below.

I was falling, falling, and then suddenly:

Wham!—I hit the outer shell of the Omega dome and was looking up as a jet of blue flame roared out of the portal above me, shooting a hundred feet out into the distance.

The outer wall of the dome was curved like the surface of a ball. I wasn't falling straight down, I was slipping down a radical curve, like riding a big water slide.

I spread out my arms and legs in the hopes of slowing down, but it didn't help. I hit bottom with a bone-jarring crash, nearly crushing the bodies of Todd and Elena, resting below.

For a second I just sat there, dazed, as Jack and Toni slid down beside me. No sooner had they touched down than they were on their feet, scooping Todd off the ground, slinging one of his arms over each of their shoulders.

"This is no time to rest, Ethan," Toni shouted at me. "Grab Elena. This whole place is one big bomb waiting to blow!"

Rising unsteadily to my feet, I picked Elena up in a fireman's carry, then lumbered as fast as I could after the others.

We hadn't gone three hundred feet before the explosion came.

_____ Chapter 21

Jack

I lay on my back, looking up at the remains of the Omega base. It looked like a Christmas ornament that someone left in a microwave on high. Enormous shards of metal, some hundreds of feet tall, lay smoldering in every direction. A plume of smoke a half mile wide and ten times as high rose slowly into the afternoon sky.

Idly I wondered how long it would be before the rats came to pick my bones clean. I had other questions on my mind, too. For example, was I broken? And if so, in how many pieces? A little voice told me that I should try to stand up and walk around, but it was shouted out by a big angry voice that said, Don't move a muscle; it hurts too much.

So I lay there.

Finally I heard another voice. A boy's voice. "Is everyone okay?" he asked. Ethan.

"Define 'okay,'" I grunted.

I realized that my arms and legs were still spread out, the way I'd landed when the bomb blast picked me up and threw me down. I propped myself into a sitting position, every muscle in my body screaming out in protest.

Ethan was staggering over to me. He held Elena Vargas's limp body in his arms. Her arms flopped lifelessly toward the ground.

I gasped. "Oh no. Is she—"

"Alive," Ethan said, laying her down gently on the ground next to me. "I don't know how, but she is." He plopped down beside her, wiping a hand across his sooty face.

"Todd, too," said Toni. She was sitting off to my right, next to the body of Todd Aldridge. Todd's chest was rising and falling with slow, easy breaths. "I'm telling you now"—Toni sniffed—"the next time we escape from an exploding building, *we* get to be the ones who sleep."

We all tried to laugh but couldn't. Instead we just sat there, staring miserably at each other with raw, bloodshot eyes.

"What a disaster," Ethan said finally. "The Omegas escaped, the time machine is gone, and we're . . ." He let the sentence die on his cracked lips.

Trapped here, I finished silently. *In the future. For good.*

The thing was, that wasn't even the worst part.

"Do you think that Ashley—that she—I mean, that *they* . . ." My voice caught in my throat.

Ethan shook his head somberly. "They're gone, Jack. Both of them. They never had a chance."

We stared at the smoking wreckage. Somewhere in there were two dead bodies. Both of them belonging to one incredible friend.

"Why are *we* alive?" Toni asked suddenly, her voice barely a whisper.

"Good question," I said.

"The dome's force shield," Ethan started to explain. "It must have contained the blast somehow. Acted like a—"

"No!" Toni screamed, her voice raw. "You don't get it! What I mean is, why are *we* alive when Ashley is *dead?* Why did we ever make her risk her life like that? What right did we have?" She was crying hard now, tears carving salty trails down her ashy cheeks. "We should *all* be dead. Not just Ashley. All of us."

By the time Toni had finished, Ethan and I were crying, too.

I guess that's why we didn't notice the footsteps.

"Gee," a voice said behind us.

I whipped around to see a girl draped in a strange yellow rubber suit.

"I hope you're not all crying over *me.* . . ."

_____ Chapter 22

Toni

"Ashley!" we all cried in unison, running up to her. "You're alive!"

I threw my arms around her neck, giving her a giant hug. "I don't believe it!" I said, tears dribbling down my face. "I thought you were dead!"

Ashley seemed a little shocked by all our attention. "Don't waste your tears on me, Toni," she told me. "You'll need them for when you see your hair."

"I don't _care_ about my hair!" I squealed in delight, and squeezed her even tighter.

"Wow. _That's_ a first," Jack cracked.

"How did you ever get out of the dome?" Ethan asked Ashley.

"Get out?" she said, looking confused. "I never even got _in._ "

Now it was our turn to look confused.

"What do you mean?" I asked, releasing her from my bear hug.

"I mean, I _tried_ to get in," she began. "But when I was in the water pipe, there was an earthquake, and the pipe collapsed in around me. My hand got caught. I remember thinking I was going to die—and that you guys were never going to get rescued—unless I got out of there somehow." She made a little laugh. "It's crazy. I even debated cutting off my arm to free myself, but then . . ."

"Then what?" I prompted.

Ashley shrugged. "I'm not sure. I must have passed out or something. I don't know how long I was unconscious, but it must have been a long time. When I woke up, I was still trapped in the pipe, but now I felt funny. Itchy all over, as if my whole body had pins and needles. And that wasn't the weirdest part."

She paused, looking embarrassed. "My clothes were gone. My shirt, my shoes, the sack with the professor's bomb—all of it. I was totally naked. And totally freaked."

Ethan and I exchanged a look.

Across from us Jack gasped, then looked at me excitedly. He was obviously coming to the same conclusion Ethan and I were. He opened his mouth to speak, but I shook my head. I wanted Ashley to finish telling her story.

By now Ashley's face had turned beet red. She went on quickly. "So there I was, still trapped in the pipe, still trying to figure a way out, only *now* wondering where my clothes went—and, more importantly, where the *bomb* went—when the explosion came. It was like another earthquake, only stronger. The force shook me free. The next thing I knew, I was hurtling back through the pipe but in the opposite direction—*away* from the dome. By the time the current died down, I'd been carried all the way back to the waterworks building."

She gestured at her strange outfit. "That's where I got this suit."

"You're lucky," I told her, smiling. "Yellow rubber is *totally* in this season."

She smiled back at me. Suddenly there were tears in her eyes. "I'm so glad to see you guys!" she gushed. "When I left the waterworks and saw all the smoke, I figured I had messed everything up. That the bomb had somehow floated down the pipe and exploded under the dome with all of you still trapped inside. But now I see you've made it out, with Todd and Elena and—"

She stopped herself short. "Where's Ashley One?" she asked, her smile fading.

Jack's eyes flickered back to me. This time I nodded at him.

"She . . . didn't make it," he said softly.

"Oh no," Ashley said.

"There's something else you need to know," Ethan said after a moment.

Ashley looked up at him, her chin quivering. "What's that?"

"Roll up your left sleeve," Ethan told her.

"My sleeve?" Ashley looked at me, obviously confused.

I smiled at her reassuringly. "Do it, Ash."

Frowning, Ashley rolled back the large rubber sleeve. A narrow pink scar was clearly visible, encircling the crook of her elbow.

Ashley blinked, then traced the thin line with her finger. "How did that—why do I—how did you know that would be there?"

"Because," Jack answered, "Ashley Two showed us a scar in the very same place."

"Ashley Two?" she said. "I don't understand. *I'm* Ashley Two."

Ethan shook his head. "No. Ashley Two died in the explosion with Ashley One," he explained to the brown-haired girl standing before us. "You . . . are Ashley *Three!*"

The sun was low on the horizon as the six of us made our slow, painful way back to Resistance headquarters. Jack and Ethan carried Todd. Ashley Three and I carried Elena.

It wasn't easy going.

"I can't believe these two slept through the *whole thing,*" Jack muttered. "It just isn't fair."

Ashley Three had been silent for most of our trek. I guess it's weird finding out you've been generated entirely from someone's arm.

Of course, *none* of us were in the mood for conversation. We all were pretty bummed.

We should have been riding the Omega time machine

back to the past. Back to our friends and families.

Instead we were right where we started.

I guess it wasn't a total loss.

I mean, even though the Omegas had escaped on the time machine, we *had* managed to destroy their base. Sure, they could return, but at least they'd have a heck of a time redecorating.

And (despite my aching arms) I had to admit it was a good thing that we'd finally rescued Elena and Todd from the Omegas' clutches.

As we crested the top of Goose Hill, Ashley Three finally spoke up.

"And so, having vanquished the evil foe, our brave heroes ride triumphantly into the sunset," she announced, making her voice sound all dramatic, like the narrator of a movie.

She giggled. Then her giggle became a chuckle. Then her chuckle became an all-out laugh.

It *was* pretty funny. We were probably the most pathetic-looking heroes ever to walk the planet. Six sore people covered in black soot, two of them passed out cold and one of them dressed like a walking rubber duckie.

Soon we all were laughing.

"Hey," Ethan said. "Isn't this the part of the movie where we learn the moral of the story?"

"And what would that be?" I asked.

"How about, 'Don't play with nuclear weapons'?" Jack offered.

"Or, 'Stay out of pipes'?" Ashley Three chimed in.

"'Sleeping thirteen-year-olds are heavy'?" I volunteered.

"No—I've got it," Ethan said. He paused for dramatic effect, looking meaningfully at Ashley Three: "'Nothing's impossible.'"

Nothing's impossible.

It was a comforting thought.

And I sure hoped it was true.

Because if we ever wanted to get out of this place—away from this nightmare world and back to the homes and the people we loved—it looked like we'd have to *achieve* the impossible.

But if an entire person could grow from someone's arm, I had a feeling that we could make that unlikely journey.

Nothing's impossible, I repeated to myself. *Sounds good to me.*

About the Author

Chris Archer grew up in New Jersey, where he spent most of his childhood wishing he had special powers.

He now divides his time between New York City and Los Angeles, California. When Chris is not writing books and screenplays, he enjoys going to scary movies, playing piano (badly), and reading suspense novels.

He has never been to Wisconsin.